crosstown

crosstown

richard scrimger

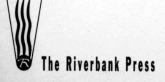
The Riverbank Press

Canadian Cataloguing in Publication Data

   Scrimger, Richard, 1957 —
      Crosstown

   ISBN 1-896332-01-3

   I. Title

PS8587.C745C76 1996   C813'.54   C96-930597-4
PR9199.3.S37C76 1996

First published in Canada by
The Riverbank Press
369 Shuter Street
Toronto, Ontario M5A 1X2

Printed and bound in Canada by Webcom

to Bridget

I would like to thank:

Dean Cooke, for perseverance against his better judgement.

John Terauds and Attila Berki, for expedition.

My parents, for their generosity.

Last night they beat me up again. Three, four of them, I don't know. Young guys with short hair, real short, like skulls they looked. I remember that. Was a time when all the guys who beat you up had long hair. Fashion. They don't take my money, don't even look, just knock me down and start kicking. Running shoes they wear, I remember thinking, thank Christ for running shoes before I go away.

I come back to blindness and the call of birds. Harsh croaking horrible old birds, sound like a flock of hanging judges. Birds like that steal your eyes when you're asleep, perch on your chest with their hard orange feet to pick a couple of dripping sloe berries. Maybe that's what happened to my eyes. I reach up. No, they're just swollen shut. I pry them open, not that I want to see. I'm lying in a bush in the park, bright yellow flowers all around me and a smell of spring. The ravens are having a discussion on the grass nearby. I must have crawled here after they beat me up. I don't remember.

First things first, I have to pee. Then I sit up and think about getting home. The ravens fly away.

It's good not to be cold. Cold days you worry all the time, collecting rags and trying to remember where the hot-air vents are. It's distracting. Yesterday was warm too, wasn't it. Soon I won't even be thinking about being cold. Of course that's when it'll freeze again. Seasons are tricky things.

My eyes stay open by themselves now. I'm walking down a busy street I don't recognize right away, which happens a lot, gas station old brick storefronts, fruit in the window video rentals black metal railing, curb chartered accountants. Darn right, too. The sign says Gerrard Street. Fair enough. There's a narrow cross-street lined with trees and parked cars and houses with locked doors. Away in the distance the tall white towers of St Jamestown stand like rotten teeth. I turn down the next street, Seaton it should be except they've taken the sign away, so it's just the street with the blind corner and the crosswalk. Sure enough, a couple of minutes later I see my friend Pete. He's standing outside the front door of the mission, like always.

Hi, Pete, I say. Where's everyone. Pete doesn't say anything.

Have they all gone, Pete. Am I too late for breakfast.

Pete doesn't say anything. Neither does the pigeon on his head. I guess breakfast is over. Missing a meal doesn't mean much today. Sometimes hunger is an animal in my stomach, with claws. Today all I have is a little hollow feeling, like a sandcastle after the tide comes in.

"Hey you! Get out of here!"

It's a mister. They all talk to me like that. This one has a tool belt and a yellow hat. I say, Sorry mister, and get out of his way. There are lots of misters around. Some are carrying big sheets of plywood, others are pointing, showing where the plywood should go, I guess. Some are standing around. A big truck is backing over the curb. I don't see anyone I know. Usually there's someone hanging around. Someone besides Pete.

"Out of the way!"

Two of them, one with plywood and one with L-shaped frames nailed together. I say, Sorry mister, and move along a bit. My throat's itchy and my tongue has started to swell. I'm thirsty.

"Mitchell!" That's my name. Someone is calling me. I turn around.

"What are you doing here?" asks Sally. She works at the mission, serving food, turning the lights off and on. She's okay. Usually she has a smile pasted on but not now.

"What happened to your face? Were you in a fight?"

No no, I say. Well it wasn't a fight, was it, a fight has two sides.

"I thought you were with the others," she says. "I didn't see you this morning but I just assumed you got on the bus with everyone else."

I'm thirsty. Yesterday I had a five. I wonder if it's still in my pocket, but I don't want to pull it out in front of Sally. I walk away. She follows, talking about what they're going to do with me. "I don't have a car," she says, "and I can't ask St Joe's to send the bus back for one person. You see that, don't you?" I say, Yes.

With a five I could manage a mickey of White Satin and still have enough for some T-bird tomorrow. Forward planning. Or Aqua Velva. Bye then, Sally, I say. Maybe I'll see you tonight.

"Haven't you been listening?" She pulls my arm. She's shouting, her earnest face all worked up. "Don't you realize that you can't come back to St Peter's tonight, or any other night. Look around you. They're tearing the mission down!"

The sheets of plywood have writing on them. DEMOLITION. I didn't notice. I say, Oh.

"We've been talking about it for months now. I saw you yesterday — remember? You promised to get your things together. You said you'd be ready to move this morning with everyone else."

I say, Oh. She goes on for a while. I'm thinking about my stuff. Probably Roscoe took it all. The big coat won't fit him, but Roscoe isn't the dressiest guy in the world. Come to think of it, the coat doesn't fit me either.

And I'm thinking about Pete. He missed the bus too.

Sally is writing something on a card. She always carries a bunch of cards with her. "This," she hands it to me, "is where you'll be going. You can read, can't you. Read it back to me."

St Joseph's Mission, I read out. Sunnyside Avenue.

"What's wrong? You turned white there, like you were going to faint. Are you ill?"

No no, I'm fine, I say.

"Okay. Flag a cab and show that address to the driver. You'll probably have to show some money too. I can give you ..." Sally is looking up the street. "No, wait," she says, waving. "This is a better way."

Things are moving too quickly for me. I'm used to that. I yawn. A cab pulls up. Sally opens the door.

"No way," says the driver when he sees me. "He'll stink up the cab." Critics.

She hands him a twenty. "That's on top of the fare," she says, giving him another. "This will cover the trip to St Joe's." She tells him the address. The driver looks at me like I'm a rat raisin in his porridge. I'm thinking, why didn't she give me the money. A week of White Satin at least.

"Goodbye, Mitch," she says, folding me into the cab.

"He going to get sick?" the driver asks her. She shakes her head. I settle back onto soft forgiving springs and we're off.

The vinyl seat cover is warm and smooth against my skin. We pass a long line of parked cars, I can see them out of the window. Their yellow parking tickets flutter in the breeze like flags. We take a corner pretty hard and I slide a bit. Now I can see signs, NO PARKING, NO STANDING, NO — something.

Sunnyside is all the way across the city, over by High Park. I wonder what it'll be like living there. About the same as here, I expect. Maybe I'll get a bottom bunk. I swallow a couple of times, try not to think about whisky wine or vodka. Or Kiwi shoe polish.

I see trees and telephone poles and the tops of houses. And

patches of sky so bright I have to close my eyes. I keep them closed until the cab driver throws me out. By the time I get up he's vanished around the corner in a puff of exhaust and I'm standing in front of a hoarding marked DEMOLITION. It takes me a minute, but I work it out. I'm back at the mission. The cabbie took the money for a crosstown trip and drove me around the block. What a person. I'm glad I peed in his car.

What now. Making my own way over to St Joe's could take me the rest of my life. Meantime I'm thirsty. I decide to ask Mack for advice. He works at the liquor store around the corner on Queen Street. A guy smart enough to stock the White Satin at eye-level is bound to have a worthwhile opinion, I figure.

That's when I notice Pete. They've knocked him over and he's lying on the grass in dusty stone pieces, his head over there, bare foot over there, hand with the keys in it over there.

Hey Pete, I say, you don't look so good. He doesn't say anything.

The misters come over. "You still here?" they say. "Beat it."

So long Pete, I say.

"What was that?" Two of them, towering over me.

I was talking to him, I say. I pick up my feet. It's been a long time between drinks.

walk and walk, taking the turns, trying not to step in the dogshit. I walk and walk and can't find Mack's. The corner with the gas station is Jarvis. I've gone too far. I turn back but I still don't see it. There's the clothes place, there's the donut place, there's the pop and candy and glue place. And there's the place where they found what was her name last winter. What was her name. Anyway Mack's should be somewhere around here, and it isn't. A kid is walking by. Red sweater and corduroy pants. Hey kid, I say, where's Mack's. The kid stares at me with his head to one side and his thumb in his mouth, kind of shy. What happened to Mack's place, I ask.

"Donald!" A loud voice from behind me. "Donald, come here!" I turn around as fast as I can. The kid scampers past me. I keep turning. By now the kid is hanging onto mom's hand and she's saying, "Don't you ever talk to people like that!"

People like what. Ah well, here's Mack himself coming out of the pop place. He's unwrapping a pack of cigarettes. I hurry over.

"Oh hi, soldier," he says. He calls everyone soldier. Saves time I guess. He puts a cigarette in his mouth, offers me one. I shake my head. "I didn't think I'd see you again. Where are you off to now?" he asks me.

Your place, I say, same as you. Only I can't find it.

"What, the liquor store? You know I don't work there anymore. They retired me last week. I bought all you soldiers a free drink. D'you not remember?" He points. "There's the place, with the brown paper in the windows."

I've passed by it two or three times already. I didn't recognize it. "They're renovating," he says. "Place was falling to bits. Whole neighbourhood's changing, what with St Peter's getting torn down and all." He lights his cigarette and throws the match away. Opens the door of the car in front of him. "Speaking of which," he says, "how come you're still here, soldier? I heard all you boys were gone."

I try to explain about missing the bus, about me and Pete missing the bus, and now Pete's gone too, broken into bits.

"So you're all alone, eh? That's too bad."

I can't say anything. I have to swallow. Mack stares at me for a bit, then shakes his head. "Well, good luck, soldier," he calls, and gets in the car.

I wander over to the liquor store. There's some writing on the brown paper. OPENING SOON. How soon, I wonder. I'm very thirsty. I knock but no one comes. After a bit I knock again, press my ear to the door. I can't hear anything. I try the door. Maybe they're already open. They aren't. I slump in the doorway. I'll wait for them to open.

A car pulls up. Looks familiar. Mack gets out. "I thought you'd still be here," he says, and then, "Look, soldier. Where do you want to go? I heard they were moving you guys to the

West End someplace — that true? I'll give you a lift, if you like."

I stare at him. Shake my head. Can't talk. Can't think. All I know is I'm thirsty.

"Damn." He's frowning. It's all around his cigarette, the frown. "You can't tell me, can you? You poor bastard, you probably don't even know." He waits a minute, then goes around and opens the trunk of the car, takes out a brown paper bag and hands it to me. "It's all I can do," he says. "It's all I can think to do." He coughs. Cigarette choking him probably. Horrible things, cigarettes. I'm glad I gave them up.

I'm dreaming. There's a bottle in the paper bag.

"It's twenty years old," he says. "Hope you like it." He gets back in the car and drives off with a roar. Not that I'm watching. I hear the roar as I sneak down the alley behind the clothes place and duck under the loading platform. The shadows are long and snaky and the ground is hard. No one's around. It might be Sunday, it's so quiet.

The bottle does look strange. For a minute I'm worried, what if it's olive oil or something. Then, in the middle of a lot of words and numbers that don't mean much, I see COGNAC in old-fashioned writing. So that's all right. But now I'm having trouble getting it open. There's wax or something all around the top. You'd think they didn't want you to drink it.

Too bad for them.

She looked so young: closer to childhood than womanhood. This was someone's daughter, someone's friend from home economics class. Not a siren or succubus; certainly not a mom. I saw girls not much younger every day, embarrassed, proud of their new calendars, relieved at being normal, talking in whispers about pads and belts and when *it* happened for the first time. She wore a cool and composed expression like a new shade of lipstick, wondering if it would suit. A round little doll face framed by a surprisingly severe haircut, long limbs held quiet in repose. Casual clothes that she wore well; she was a model. Leon Opara was proud of his daughter, the model. He'd told me so. Magda's so independent, he said. Never had a mother to tie her down.

Leon Opara sat on more boards — hospital, clinic, charity, faculty — than he had fingers to count them on and had more preferments in his vest pocket than pens. You didn't ignore a request from him if you wanted to get ahead. And I did want to get ahead. I wanted more privileges at the Civic Hospital — more space on the third floor, more time in the operating room. I wanted to be Chief of Obstetrics. Cochrane was in his fifties and he wasn't going to be around forever. So when Opara himself phoned to request an appointment for his daughter that afternoon, I made room for her as if she'd been an emergency case. In effect she was an emergency: a career emergency.

Her father explained her situation in quiet club tones while she looked on, remote and a bit apprehensive. Of course, I'd known as soon as she came in. What I didn't understand was why they'd come to me. I brought up the point gently. Naturally, I'd be honoured to consult with her family doctor on the case, I said.

"Actually, I was hoping for more than consultation, Dr Mitchell. Magda's own doctor is a little conservative. And he doesn't do any surgery."

In that case, I said, he and I could work together to —

"No." Opara didn't let me finish. "I want you, Mitchell. I've heard great things about your operating technique. And you're still young. McKendrick — that's Magda's family doctor — is an excellent man, but I didn't want to trouble him with this kind of thing." Opara flushed slightly but kept his eyes on me. "My late wife's maiden name was O'Neill. It's a fairly common name. I was hoping that, in the interests of discretion ..." his voice trailed away.

Oh, I said.

That was the point. Discretion. Opara wasn't suggesting anything illegal. At that time abortion was not a criminal act in Ontario, provided it was done for genuine medical reasons. But it wasn't like having your wisdom teeth out. Opara was a well-known man. He didn't want gossip columnists at his daughter's bedside. He didn't want sympathy from his buddies in the boardroom. He wanted an unknown doctor who could do the job and keep his mouth shut.

How do you feel about it, Magda, I asked. That was the name I'd put at the top of the file.

"Dad says that you can ... help me, doctor." A high voice, thin and empty of emotion. Did she realize what was going on.

I'd like you to tell me exactly what you want me to do, I said.

"I want an abortion."

I nodded, told her it was a very serious step for her.

"Serious." She nodded too. Was she mimicking me. Opara frowned. She fumbled with a pack of cigarettes.

What about your partner. Your boyfriend. Does he know what you're planning, I asked. She shrugged. I pressed the point. Does he know, I said. You should tell him, Magda. It's his responsibility too. She shrugged again. Fifteen-year-olds are very good at conveying lack of interest. The unlit cigarette hung in her mouth. I leaned across the desk with my lighter.

Her father sat very still. I took a deep breath and tried not to look at him. Okay, Magda, I said, I think I can agree to do this. She nodded. Her hair swung stiffly, like chin straps on an old football helmet. Before we go any further I'd like to examine you, I said. Why don't you go next door. The nurse will tell you what to do. I'll be with you in a moment.

When she was gone Opara sat back in his chair. I hadn't realized he was tense until he relaxed. "Will the committee object?" he said. Every procedure had to be approved beforehand by a panel of doctors.

I shrugged. She's fifteen, unfit for motherhood, depressed — not an unusual scenario, I said. They'll recommend counselling. It might even be a good idea.

"Will they have to see her?"

I said I didn't think so. They'd trust my opinion.

"Good." He didn't say that some of the committee — old Cochrane for instance — would no doubt recognize Leon Opara's darling daughter, but that's what he was thinking. "When can you do it?" he asked.

The sooner the better; we both knew that. If there are no complications I could operate a week Monday, I said.

"Eleven days." He wasn't happy.

Mind you, I said, taking my luck in both hands and pulling hard, if I had the hospital board's authorization for another place in Three E — that's the GYN ward — I could probably fit Magda in on Tuesday or Wednesday of next week. It's a matter of space, I said. I'm still a new boy.

His eyes met mine. "As it happens," he said, "I'm lunching with two members of your Medical Affairs Committee tomorrow. I'll mention your name. Favourably. I think I can promise you the space."

As simple as that. He stood up when I did and held out his hand. "Thank you, Mitchell," he said, smiling. "I won't forget this."

I smiled back. I won't let you, I said.

How far along are you, I asked her.

She thought about it. At least I assumed she was thinking. There was no movement, no expression on her beautiful face. "Three months ... four maybe."

I asked if she'd checked her calendar; was she sure of her dates. She was young and fit and this was her first pregnancy. At sixteen weeks I wouldn't have expected more than a little thickening, but there was a decided bulge below the navel. I'd have said she was at least four months gone. You had your last period in ... December, I said. She nodded. I finished the examination quickly.

You're a healthy young woman and I'm sure everything is going to be fine, I said. You've got nothing to worry about. She didn't look at me. Was she bored. I'm going to book a sonogram — that's a routine check — for you tomorrow, I said. Right now I'm going to go over a few things, so that you know what's going to happen next week. I outlined the procedure briefly. She didn't seem to be paying attention. I realized then that she wasn't bored. She was terrified.

I put my arm around her shoulders and told her again not to worry, that she was in good hands, that in a couple of weeks she could go back to her regular life as if nothing had happened.

She burst into tears. So much for my bedside manner.

wake up wet. Not from the rain. Damn. I get to my feet. I'm wet all down my pants. Not the cognac. Damn. I used to wake up crying. This is the first time I've pissed myself. I hope it doesn't become a habit.

Footsteps come down the alley towards me, flap flap flap. Doesn't sound like Roscoe. Could be what is his name, the Swede with big ears, or maybe Jimmy. I check the bottle. There's a little bit left at the bottom. No there isn't. I swallow nothing. Did I drink it or spill it. The steps get closer. Someone muttering in a high voice. Not the Swede or Jimmy. It's getting darker now and I can't see who it is, just a couple of legs and a coat on the ground. He's being sick. There there, I say. He looks up. A kid with a skull haircut. He's unhappy. I move on. My front is starting to dry.

Cars have their lights on. There's the clothes place and the cigarette and bitters place. Wonder where Mack's is. Must have passed it. Keep going. People ignore me. It's something I'm used to, not being there. Sorry mister, I say, ducking out of the way at the intersection. He goes by in a swirl of topcoat. A lamppost appears. I walk around it. I'm looking forward to dinner. It feels like dinner time outside, the right kind of light, the sense of purpose that most people have going home. Mornings, they look different. Just as busy, but different. Another lamppost. Up ahead a blind girl is feeling for the curb with her stick. She wants to cross. No one is helping her. I hurry forward and take her arm. Let me, I say.

"Thanks," she says, clear and willing. To me. "Thanks." I start to lead her, but halfway across she shakes herself free. "What is this? Who are you?"

Come on, I say, only a bit farther.

"What's that smell?" When you lose one sense the others become keener, don't they. "It's you! You stink!"

Yes, I say, and you're blind. But I can always take a bath. Come on now.

She screams. "Help! Someone help!" Heads turn. Traffic stops. Car doors open. Now that she's being taken care of everyone wants to help her.

I cut across the intersection and down the street, Seaton is it, or George. There's a tennis court behind a chain-link fence. Jimmy found a racket there once but they wouldn't let him bring it into the mission, called it an offensive weapon. Obviously never saw him play.

Keep going. Maybe it'll be macaroni tonight. Macaroni's good and not too complicated to eat. I'm so hungry right now I could even eat the cat stew, I know they call it veal, but that's what it tastes like, and Roscoe says he's heard them making it. Wednesday's macaroni. It's all written down and posted. Wednesday's macaroni — unless it's Friday. Sally tells me I'd know what was for dinner if I remembered the schedule. Yes, I say, and if I knew what day of the week it was.

Oh my God, I forgot. I stare at the hoarding. Already it's covered with pictures of lions and fat ladies, telephone numbers and slogans. Blank sheets of plywood don't stand a chance, do they. No dinner. Probably wasn't macaroni anyway, I tell myself, and my hunger settles gently into sand. People pass by. They don't stop to look at me. They don't stop to look at the pictures or the writing on the hoarding. Lots of people. I close my eyes and they keep coming, I can see them inside my head moving away, getting smaller and smaller as they move further and further inside me, smaller and smaller and smaller.

I hear someone saying, "Get away from that." I feel something warm and wet. "Did you hear me, Blackie? Get away from — what is that, anyway?" I hear panting. "Oh, my God! It's a dead body." Compliments. The panting goes away.

I hear someone else. "The tip was wrong. He's alive, all right. He may wish he wasn't. Come on, you, on your feet." A light in my eyes. Hands, rough but not mean, pulling me up.

"You'll have to get a move on, now."

Okay, I say. Cops aren't misters.

"Should we run him in, Fred?" An eager voice.

"For what? Mumbling? Sleeping on the job? Having shit on him? Hell, we'd have to run in most of city council."

Shit on him. Thanks Blackie.

"Well, what do we do then? We can't just leave him here."

Light again. I blink and turn away. "With St Pete's gone we're going to be seeing more guys like him," says Fred. "It'll take a while before they move on. You know, it's hard to tell, but I think this one's sober. Or close. Are you, buddy? Are you straight?"

I say the first thing that comes into my mind.

"Macaroni?" says Junior. "You hear that, Fred. He said macaroni."

Now that I've said it out loud, I realize how hungry I am.

"Hey, buddy," says Fred. "When was the last time you ate?" I shake my head. "Don't know? I thought so. Come on. This way." He marches me to the patrol car. It's about four feet away. Cops hate walking.

"We running him in after all?"

"No." Fred puts me in back and gets in the driver's side.

Junior gets in the other side. "Phew," he says. Fred doesn't say anything. He starts the car. "If we're not taking him to the station, where are we taking him?" Junior wants to know.

Fred turns a corner onto a busy street, King, I think. I count the blocks — three, four, five. I lose count. We turn onto a quieter street. No trees or houses, just big dark buildings with fences around them, vacant lots filled with rubble, bare bulbs that don't work, narrow laneways leading to who knows what. Cosy. Fred stops the car and turns around.

"Listen to me," he says through the safety mesh. "You can't go back. There's no place for you back there. Stay out of the old neighbourhood. I'm telling you this for your own good. They don't want you there. Understand?"

I nod my head. He gets out and opens my door from the outside. "It's too late to find you a place to sleep tonight. There's a church up the street a couple of blocks. You can try there in the morning. Now, out of the car."

He has a big greasy bag in his free hand. I take it. Thanks, I say. Junior protests. "But, Fred, that's our dinner."

Fred doesn't answer. The smell of corned beef is on his hands and mine. It links us together. He tells me good luck "And remember," pulling me close so that I see him clearly for the first time — a big man with hair like iron filings and an expression to match, "don't try to go back. If I see you in my precinct again, I'll hurt you."

And this one is the good cop.

I clutch the bag. They drive away. I look for someplace dark and quiet.

n the morning things are clearer, a bit. I'm around the back of a warehouse, lying on a stack of cardboard boxes, used boxes from the look of them. Not fruit or vegetable boxes, it's not that kind of warehouse. Aluminum siding or machine tools or something. Comfortable and clean. The bag with the cops' dinner is gone and I'm not hungry. I must have eaten it. Beside me is a doorstep. That's handy.

When I'm finished I stretch like an arthritic cat, and try to think what I'll do now. It's early, sun's just up. I can't hear anything. There's a barbed-wire fence a few feet away. On the other side is a vacant lot. I wonder where I am.

There's a tickle at the back of my throat, a reminder, like a dumb little tune you can't quite forget. I'm not thirsty yet, but I will be soon. I belch. Corned beef all right.

Things are quiet. Maybe it's Sunday. I try to work back, but the last Sunday I can be sure of had a turkey in it, and that was a while ago. I lie down again — you know, cardboard is kind of comfortable. There's some blue in the sky and the morning is almost warm and I haven't been beaten up in a while. Paradise. I try to ignore the tickle in my throat.

"Hey you!"

A man is pointing a gun at me. He's nervous. The gun shakes. "Get out of here! I mean it." He's an older guy with a bad complexion, dressed in black, spit polish on his boots. Billy the Codger. Behind him a young woman is frowning.

"For heaven's sake put that away, Lester. You look ridiculous," she says. I agree. "I asked you to escort him off the premises, not lynch him."

Lester pouts. "He could be dangerous," he says.

"Only if he breathes on you." A nice lady. Lester lowers his gun. "Now you," she says to me. "Get off the lot."

I nearly say, Yes Mister. I scramble to my feet and shuffle away. Lester trails after me. I'm wondering why she has him around at all.

There's a small gate set into the wire fence. Lester walks me up to it and then pushes me through the opening onto the sidewalk. Well-kept sidewalk, poured last year. I know because my head is only an inch away from the stamp. "And don't come back," he calls.

I climb to my feet. Wind's from the bottom today, brings the waterfront smell with it. Been a while since I was down there. Gulls, landfill, empty warehouses mostly. It's like that right across the bottom of the city except for a bit in the middle where they take all the pictures. That's where you can see sailboats, floating restaurants, guys in white pants.

Up ahead is a wide street with a familiar name. Queen. I turn my back to the rising sun and keep walking.

The first transit shelter I come to says Bellamy Street. Never heard of it. I walk along, checking the places. Shoes in one window, then a picture of a sandy beach, then steam – a dry cleaner. Then cans of food. Then an empty doorway – no, someone's propped against the back corner. Her eyes are wide open and her jaw is pushed out as if to say, So what.

I stop. Hi, I say. A truck rumbles by. She nods but I can't hear if she says anything. Where is this, I ask. She doesn't answer. Maybe I'm too vague. Maybe she doesn't know either. She has a shopping bag full of stuff in one hand.

I don't know my way around here, I say. Where can a guy get a meal. And maybe a bed.

Still no answer. She looks like she's ready to say something but it doesn't come out. A streetcar passes, making the windows rattle. She nods her head again. This time she loses her balance and falls right over. Her head hits the sidewalk a pretty good whack but she doesn't change her expression. Oh.

I wonder what's in the shopping bag.

People are walking past the doorway, not looking, full of breakfast and their own troubles. I step towards the body, take the bag easily. Rigor has passed, she must be a day gone at least, I think. Three, four doorways down I see a pair of shoes sticking out. I think about stopping. He's asleep and they're better shoes than mine. But I'm more interested in what's in the bag.

Where can I go. This isn't my territory, Queen and whatever it is. I don't know where the alleys are, the nooks and blind corners, and back lots that no one bothers with. I take the first turning and duck round behind a store. A mister is unloading something from a truck. He looks at me. I back out. Careful with the bag. The next alley leads to a parking lot. Two cars have their motors running. I turn and turn again, who was that, Dick Turpin wasn't it, and keep going until I get to a pizza outlet. The sign on the corner says Mutual Street. Then up ahead I see a church. Like most churches this one is built with lots of spare bits sticking out, so there's plenty of shadow. I duck down the side under the stained-glass windows, find my own bit of dark and open the bag.

I thought so. I'd felt its weight. That's why I was careful not to bump into anything. Inside the bag, under some clothes and a nearly dead kitten, is a bottle. I pull it out. Red. I don't recognize the brand. Courage, it's called. Why not.

I dump the bag. Nothing more of interest. The kitten makes some kind of mewing sound as it lies there on the pavement. The bottle opens easily and lets me inside.

My wife came from money — sounds like a different country, doesn't it. Her grandfather returned from the First World War to build the biggest tool and die fitter in the province. "Named it CMR after his old regiment, the Canadian Mounted Rifles. And we've been in business ever since," her father told me the first time I met him — and several more times afterwards. He never told me what a tool and die fitter was.

Lucy grew up in Rosedale, the rich heart of Toronto where old WASP fortunes pile up like autumn leaves. Cardigans and country clubs, pedigree dogs and pigs-in-a-blanket, private schools and European holidays. Easy to make fun of, and they don't mind a bit because they know it's all envy. I was too overwhelmed to be envious that first evening. If Lucy hadn't been at the door to meet me I'd have shaken hands with the butler.

She had shown up in the Emergency Room a few months earlier, spitting mad at the tailgater who had totalled her motorcycle. I'd been able to make her laugh, set her broken leg and put her to sleep. Then I'd seen her the next day on rounds with a bunch of other residents. The doctor in charge picked me to demonstrate bedside manner.

Does this hurt, Miss Watson, I said softly, staring into her eyes. They were dark and liquid, like maple syrup, but her face was no pancake. She had a high-bridged nose, small perfect teeth and a firm chin. Her hair fell in a chestnut wave. Or this.

"Mitchell," the doctor snapped, "that's her good leg. The cast, you may have noticed, is on the other one." I ignored him.

Sometimes, Miss Watson, we get what's called sympathetic pain. Typically it occurs here in the good leg, I said. That's what the doctor called it and I agree with him — it's a good leg.

"No pain," she said. "No pain at all."

That's great, I told her. We smiled. The other residents were acting like I'd farted in church. The doctor — what was his name — was so mad he made me prep the next three surgeries. Gave me a hell of a chewing out. You're right, sir, I said. Completely unprofessional. Don't know what came over me. Never happen again. Yes sir, I said, I'll go back to her room and apologize.

That first dinner creaked along like a maiden aunt in a bath chair. Lucy's parents insisted I call them Arthur and Lillian, which made me feel awkward when I forgot. They recounted anecdotes and talked about gardens and relatives. When I couldn't join in they asked me personal questions. My father's dead, I said. My mother works in a supermarket. I was raised a Catholic. No, I don't go to church any more. I'm twenty-six. Actually, I just got a haircut. I'm specializing in obstetrics and gynecology. I'm afraid

I don't have a lot of influential friends, unless — I put on a winning smile — you'd like to count yourselves.

Arthur murmured vaguely. Lillian smiled right back at me. "I'm sure we wouldn't presume on such short acquaintance," she said. Lucy, sitting across from me, looked like she was going to say something, but didn't. Her father began another anecdote, a set piece with a punch line that hove into view like a ship in a fog bank. I tried to laugh appreciatively.

Dessert was baked pudding and sauce. I dropped my helping onto the floor and upset the silver sauceboat all over Arthur's. Forgive me, I said, I really am very — and I paused, trying to find the right word.

"Clumsy?" Lillian suggested. "Yes. What a pity you've chosen a career in obstetrics, Mitchell. Babies require even more careful handling than sauceboats."

I lit a cigarette after dinner from sheer nervousness, I didn't even know what I was doing. I looked around for an ashtray and saw Arthur's frown instead.

"Use your saucer," Lucy suggested.

"What a silly suggestion, my dear," said her mother. "We don't usually smoke in this room, Mitchell, because the tapestry behind you is rather fragile. But if you'd really like your cigarette I'm sure Grover can bring you an ashtray." No no, I mumbled, turning a rich oven-baked red. I dropped the cigarette in my coffee. Arthur's frown was replaced by a perplexed expression.

Thanks so much for having me, Mrs Watson — I mean, Lillian, I said, shaking hands. It was only nine-thirty, but they didn't want me there and neither did I, and why should we all have a bad time.

"It's always an — interesting experience to meet Lucy's friends." She permitted herself a small sigh.

"Where are you going, my dear?" Arthur asked his daughter, who had put on a denim jacket she didn't need in this weather. She looked great, though.

"I'm going to drive Mitchell home."

"How'd he get here? Why can't he go home the way he came?" Nothing like good old Toronto hospitality.

"I want to drive him, dad."

"That's right, Arthur. Lucy and Mitchell want to enjoy some time together. You run along, dear, but remember the MacGilli- vrays are coming to brunch tomorrow and they do so like to see you looking your best."

In the car she apologized for her parents. "They're from another age."

Do you mean the Stone Age, I said, or the Ice Age.

"They may be old-fashioned, but I'm their only child and they want what's best for me. It's rather sweet, really." And her jaw clamped shut.

What do *you* want, I said.

Did I say the car was a sports convertible? Lucy drove through Rosedale's maze of stately homes and along Bloor Street like a rally champ, leaving the sedate early-evening traffic in her rear-view mirror. She wore driving gloves with soft black leather palms. I paid particular attention to her right hand as it manipulated the shift lever through the gearbox with hypnotic intensity. Up and down went the gloved hand, tugging this way and that while the engine moaned and growled. She liked resting her palm on the knob of the lever to settle it in neutral, then she'd coax it into gear, teasing it with her fingertips before pulling in earnest, harder, harder, second, third, all the way into top, with the car responding, faster, louder, her lips parted, hair flying, skirt riding up her thighs as she worked the clutch and accelerator, pulse and revolutions way up. Mine too.

She ran a stale yellow light at Bathurst Street and then had to brake hard for a red at Palmerston Avenue, yanking the stick back to neutral. I could see it quivering in her hand.

"Right now," she said, "I want you." Take the next left, I said.

"I don't know what I want." She stared up at the ceiling of my junior one-bedroom apartment. Cracks in the plaster, furniture from Goodwill, rent cheque on the dresser, due tomorrow. "I don't want the York Club, I don't want CMR Tool and Die Fittings, I don't want London Paris Zurich and Vienna. I'm twenty-two and I live with my parents. I draw and sail and play tennis. I know all about mitosis and square roots and the movement for Responsible Government in Upper and Lower Canada. What do I want, Mitchell? You tell me."

I stood beside the bed with two popsicles in my hand. I was almost a doctor. I knew all the answers. You want orange, I said. I'll take banana.

The wedding was at St Paul's Anglican, the heart of WASP Toronto spiritual life. Early springtime, crocuses and forsythia and the last of the slush. The streets teemed with elderly ladies in elastic button boots. My mother frowned all through the service, then left abruptly. Lucy's relations filled both sides of the church. Every one of them told me how lucky I was. None of them told Lucy how lucky she was.

Lots of shadows around a church but you can't hide in them for long. Someone always finds you. Priest or janitor, sometimes another poor bugger like yourself. Try to avoid the janitors.

"Come on, son. Come on." He's squatting, hitting me between the shoulder blades, shaking me back and forth. I feel like a can of pop at a picnic. I can't breathe. I don't feel very well. Horrible stuff she was drinking, whoever she was — probably killed her. I try to keep it down. Can't.

"That's better. You had me worried for a moment there." Not a janitor. Vomit all over his shoe but he's smiling. He's younger than I am, big soft eyes like a donkey. "How do you feel now?"

I'm all right, I say, sitting up slowly. He's not a mister. Misters don't wear cassocks. Misters don't call you son.

"Can you stand?" Offering one hand. There's a kitten in the other one. I get halfway up, stagger. He grabs me by the back of my coat. Big strong guy, holds me up like a puppet.

I'm all right, I say again. I see the bottle over there. Empty, of course.

"You must be hungry," he says, walking me towards a door in the side of the church. "Won't you join me for lunch? I was just sitting down myself when I heard this little girl here," holding up the kitten. It mews hopefully. I make a face. I've never liked cats much. "Saved your life, she did," he goes on. "I went out to get her and found you choking to death."

I feel awkward. There's something he wants me to ask him and I can't think what. How old are you, I say finally.

"Old enough to be your father," he answers, kind of solemn. For a second he almost looks it. Then he smiles and goes back to being younger than me.

You know what it smells like inside. Incense, poverty, beeswax. We're in a hallway with a strip of carpet running down the middle and doors down all one side. His door looks like the others. On his desk there's a tray with a couple of sandwiches on a chipped plate, a glass of milk and an apple. Gourmet. He sits me in one wooden chair and himself in the other. The food's between us. He puts a sandwich in front of me, takes the other for himself and pours some milk for the kitten, not hurrying. I haven't started yet. He notices and smiles. I feel like I've been tested for something, but I can't tell if I've passed or failed. He bows his head. "Bless us, O Lord, and these Thy gifts." I know this one, I know when it ends. The sandwiches are tuna fish.

"Do you want to tell me your name?" he asks when there's no more food. I tell him. His is Frank.

"I haven't seen you around here before. Do you have a place to stay?" No, I say. The kitten is asleep on the floor, its dirty white front rising and falling. The plate is licked dry.

"Would you like a place — for a little while? We have no resources here, but I can put you in touch with a shelter not too far away." I don't say anything. A bell rings somewhere.

"Are you in pain?" he asks.

No, I say. I'm full of fish and apple.

"Can I do anything to help you?"

I'd ask if he has any spare, but I know he doesn't. They never do. Priests will give you anything they have, but they don't have anything. Not like misters. Misters have lots, but won't part with any of it.

"You know, Mitchell," he says, "when I went out to rescue this kitty here, you were sleeping peacefully, smiling to beat the band. I was going to leave you alone, and then you called out a name. You were dreaming. You called out a name in your sleep and it was then that you began to choke. Do you remember?" I shake my head.

He looks at me kind of sharpish. "Who's Lucy?" he asks.

It's another test and I don't know the answer. "None of my business," he says, "but when you said her name you sounded sorry. I've heard that sound before — often. I wondered if you'd let me help you."

I sit there, staring at the cat.

"Lucy is someone you know, someone close to you," he goes on. "Maybe she let you down — maybe you let her down?" I'm not giving away much but it doesn't bother him. "Mother, sister, wife, daughter — it's usually the family things that come back to hurt us. Come on, son. Tell me about her. You're in pain," he says. "Let me help you. You know I can."

Silence, pure white silence and a smell of incense, and I belch right in the middle of it, birdshit falling onto a field of snow. I feel better. He smiles and asks me straight out, "What did you do to her?" I can't remember, I tell him.

"Try. Try now."

I've been trying, I say. Forever it seems I've been trying. I remember her and Cheryl Ann. That's my daughter, I say. I see them both, sitting in the living room. Cheryl Ann is sick. Purple slippers she's wearing, with Minnie Mouse on them. My wife is reading to her. I have to go. I'm angry and I leave.

"Go on."

I don't know why I'm so angry, I say. I take the wrong car keys, so I end up driving my wife's car. And, and ... then I don't see them.

"Why not?"

I don't see them again. I can't see them. I can't.

"What happened?"

I can't remember.

"What happened, Mitchell?" His face is close to mine. I can see the lines around his soft eyes, smell the sweat on him. No, wait a minute. That's me I smell. Impressive.

I can't remember, I say. He sits back and wipes his face.

There's a knock on the door, a tentative old-maid knock, and she enters holding a piece of paper in her hand the way she always does. I know her, thin, severe, middle-aged, plain, earnest, tongue poking out like a piece of cheese from a mousetrap of a mouth. Do I ever know her. She's good. So good it hurts.

"I'm sorry, Father Frank," she says, handling his name like her best silver. She always is sorry. "I thought you'd be alone. Hello there," to me, in the voice she uses for me. "How are you feeling today?" Fine, I say, but she's looking at him.

"Will you be much longer?"

"No," he says with a sigh. "I think we're almost done."

Something about her.

"Can I show you to the door?" she says to me. Something about her strikes a chord. She's thin but she looks awkward. She's wearing her clothes wrong. I've seen it, a long time ago. Before I think what I'm doing I say to her, Two months.

She blinks. "I beg your pardon?" she says.

I stand up. Two months, I say. Maybe a bit more. Aren't you?

Frank's on his feet too. He's paying attention.

"I don't know what you can be talking about." Her face crawls with fear.

"Mary Alice?" says Frank.

Take it easy, I say. Rest. Lie down more. At your age, and your first, you have to be careful.

"Mary Alice?" he says again.

I head for the door. She bursts into tears.

"Wait," Frank calls after me. But I'm already gone.

Of course, I turn the wrong way and can't get outside. I blunder down the long twisting hall trying knobs and handles. Everything's locked. Suspicion is a dreadful thing. I follow the strip of carpet, red as red wine, trying to find the way out. Past doors with gold numbers, up some steps, doors with black numbers, down some steps, doors with black letters, around a corner, up some more steps to a small door with nothing on it, the first one I can open. It's dark inside. The smell takes me way back — disinfectant, pink liquid soap, a certain brand of floor cleaner and those little white hockey pucks they put in the bottom of urinals. That reminds me. I feel around for something made of porcelain.

Much better now.

More stairs. Keep those old priests in good shape. I see bathroom doors, clearly marked, and wonder where I — but it sure smelled like a bathroom. I'm tired. A different carpet underfoot now, and a wider hall. Swing doors leading to you know where. It's a pretty big one, altar a long way off and a Lady Chapel to one side. Carved ceiling, statues by the pillars, speakers. Workmen at the front, preparing for something. Women at the back, praying. There always are. I find a pew out of the way and lie down, and the next thing I know I'm listening to a conversation.

"Did she come to you, Frank?"

"No, Father, that's what's so odd. I didn't suspect a thing. It was a vagrant, of all people, who noticed her condition."

My friend Frank and another priest, a couple of rows up.

"A bum? What was a bum doing in your office?"

"Sharing my lunch," says Frank.

"Oh." He sighs, like he knows all about Frank's lunch dates with vagrants. "Come to think of it, I do notice a peculiar odour about you," he says. "Not sanctity either. But how does a street person come to be an expert on obstetrics? Did he find a medical degree in a garbage can beside some fish heads? Her condition isn't obvious. She isn't glowing, or anything. Why believe what your bum says? He was probably hallucinating."

"I don't think he's an ordinary vagrant," says Frank.

"They're all ordinary."

"No, Father. I've never believed that. In fact, I'd say the reverse was true."

"He was drunk."

"No, again. And his diagnosis was never in doubt. Mary Alice confessed as soon as he left. Told me all about it."

"All?" says the other one, sharply.

"She said she'd been foolish, and was now pregnant and in distress. I tried to calm her down. It wasn't easy. I gave her the rest of the day off."

Shouldn't be listening, I suppose. None of my business. But I'm too tired to move and the pew is soft enough to sleep on.

"Father Tom," from up front. "Is everything set for the baptism?"

"No," he calls. "I promised Mrs Whitehouse that we'd use the old marble font, the one she was baptized in herself. Could you get it out of the storage room, please, Bert?"

"Yes, Father."

"Do you know," Frank asks, "if Mary Alice has ever been married? I know she isn't now, but I didn't inquire further."

"I — how should I know? I hardly know the woman." Father Tom sounds harsh. "I may have seen her occasionally, exchanged the odd word, but that is all."

Frank doesn't say anything.

"Do you think we'll have any trouble with her, Frank? The bishop won't be pleased. And if she chose to, this — Mary Alice, did you say her name was — could create a lot of bad publicity for the parish. Maybe she should take a little holiday."

"You're the pastor, Tom. What are you suggesting?"

Father Tom says something I can't hear. I'm lying back watching a ceiling fan go around and around. Like a helicopter, only with the rotor inside. I wonder how the church will ever get off the ground with this kind of engineering.

"I'm sure Mary Alice will want to talk to you," says Frank. "And if she decides to go away for a time, of course we'll understand. Try to convince her," he says, "that we're all behind her in this. A baby is a work of God. I'm sure she'll want to hear that from you, Tom."

"Why?" Father Tom has a bright, sharp voice, like polished chrome. "Why me, especially? Are you suggesting anything, Frank? Why should she want to hear about God and babies from me?"

"Because," gently, "you're her boss and her spiritual father."

I yawn wide enough to catch a pop fly, and the blood and oxygen rush to my head with a sound like galloping horses. When the, what are they, hoofbeats recede I hear a voice from far away. Swearing. I'm not shocked, of course. Hear those words every day of my life. But they do sound different in a church. Behind me the women stop muttering and clacking. Tom and Frank stand up. The swearing comes closer.

On the wall beside me is a Station of the Cross. Jesus meets his afflicted mother. She's wearing a blue robe over a brown robe. I hear a voice telling me, Don't put blue and brown together. It looks cheap. My mom's voice. She died long ago. I thought I had no memories of her. I guess I was wrong. Or it could be Roscoe's voice. Come to think of it, he never wears blue and brown together. Just brown, right down to his finger-nails. And if it didn't start brown, Roscoe only has to wait.

The doors bang open and I hear apologies. "I'm sorry, Father," he says, Bert, I guess, "but I was just in the storage room and ... somebody's gone and pissed in the old font."

I slink past the praying ladies. They're too busy to suspect me.

There's a crowd down the street from the church, waiting. I think about joining them, waiting's one of my best things, but by the time I reach them I've changed my mind. They're all excited, talking loudly and pointing, and some of them are jumping on and off the curb. It's coming, whatever it is they're waiting for. I decide to move on. Waiting suits me best when nothing's going to happen.

Farther along the street is a sofa with the stuffing showing through. It makes a perfect place to wait for nothing.

A streetcar passes by, swaying gently. A dog in a new collar sniffs and moves on. A girl passes by, tight black boots and a short skirt with nothing under it but a tattoo. Tattoo is new to me, everything else pretty much as I remember it. Spits her gum out beside me, gets into a car with dark windows. A kid with glasses stops, frowns down at me.

"Hey, mom, there's a man lying on this couch."

"Come along, dear."

"You okay?" the kid asks. I'm fine, I say.

"Come here this instant! Haven't I told you not to talk to strange people?"

Does she mean strangers. Probably not. A taxi goes by, fast, empty. Another one, slow, with a fare. A white stretch limousine glides to a stop. The back window slides down and a white glove empties a plastic scoop onto the road. Somewhere inside the car a yappy dog sounds proud of itself. The gloved hand retreats. The window slides up. The car glides away. A van pulls up on the curb, a guy gets out with a package, leaps over the couch and me and runs off. A minute later he's back. A cop car passes by. And another streetcar. Bicycle carts selling ice-cream cones pass by, and carts selling popcorn, candy apples, chestnuts and bird calls. A lady with a bundle buggy toils along real slow, calling, "Wait, wait for me," in a weak old voice. Who is she talking to. Everyone, I guess. A jogger comes by. Red shoes, Maple Leaf jersey. Number 93. Was a time 30 was the highest number, and he was the backup goalie. 93 must be the janitor's assistant. An ambulance races by, flashing and beeping. I'm wondering if there's anyone who hasn't come by yet. Give me a nun, an accordionist and the mayor and I've seen everyone in town.

And them. A gang. I forgot about them. They come piling out of the next streetcar with their skull faces, laughing at something that probably isn't funny. I wonder if I have time to get away. I could blend in with the passersby, but suddenly the street is empty except for me and them.

They've seen me. They crowd around, laughing even harder. One of them has tears in his eyes he's laughing so hard. I'm a lie-down comic. I try to stand up. Not worth the effort. The crying one kicks my feet out from under me. I fall to the sidewalk. I try to get up again, I don't know why, just for something to do. Another one of them pushes me off balance and I fall. "Timber!" he shouts. Very droll.

A mister comes by. Haven't seen one in a while. Blue topcoat with a belt. Black shoes with tassels. I'm on my knees, close enough to see that the tassels have silver at the tips. Help, mister, I say. He walks on by. Doesn't even look down. I feel a sharp pain in my ribs. I've been kicked. Not a surprise. I tense for the next one, wondering where the cops have gone to, only there isn't a next one, not for the longest time. I can't stay tensed for ever. I risk a quick look.

"Isn't she cute," says one of them.

"Look, she's chasing me shoelace," says another. They're all clustered around a little gray kitten with a white front. Looks familiar.

The one who was crying with laughter picks it up. "Hello, snookums," he says. "Want to lick my finger?"

All this time I'm trying to get up. My side hurts. It's taking me even longer than normal.

"We never had a pet before. What'll we do with the kitty?" one of them asks.

"Let's kill it."

"Yeah. We could smash it with rocks. Or string it up."

"Or drown it."

Nice kids.

"Fuck, it got away. See that — it just jumped out of me hands. Hey, come back, kitty. Where'd it go?"

I've managed to take maybe a dozen steps when I hear a hissing noise and a door opens like magic in front of me. I step inside, the door closes and off I go in the streetcar.

"Where's your ticket?" says the driver. Last time I rode the streetcar it was really cold. I figured it was worth the money to warm up. "Tickets two dollars. Exact change only." She squints down at me. I reach into my pocket.

"That's a cat," she says. I look down. It must have followed me. Not my cat, I say.

I get an idea. It feels funny, been a while since I had one. I pull a piece of paper from my pocket. The one where Sally wrote the address. Do you go, I ask, to Sunnyside Avenue.

"Pets must be on a leash or in a box," she says, slowing down.

Sunnyside Avenue, I say again. Do you go there.

"Victoria Street," she says into a microphone, then pushes the button to open the door. "Get out," she tells me, "and take your cat with you." Not my cat, I say again, but people are pushing past me to get out and I end up on the road.

I don't know where I am, of course. In front of me is a sinister, square building with dark windows. Huge metal doors open like jaws, drawing some misters inside, spitting more out. REVENUE CANADA says the sign. Lots of misters around. I walk on quickly. Getting late now, the sun has swung round so that it's shining down the street at me. People's shadows arrive a long way ahead of the people. I'm in the middle of an intersection when I notice a window across the street with a flashing light in it. The flashing light spells out BARGAINS. Well, so do most of them. But this one is shaped like a bottle.

I'm thirsty.

Horns honk. I stare attentively. Not a beer bottle, I decide.

Certainly not wine. Gin, that's what it is. A gin bottle. More horns.

"Get off the road, asshole!" Me, I guess.

I find myself walking towards the bottle. The stream of traffic parts around me. Drivers roll down their windows to yell. I don't pay any attention. I reach the bottle at last and go in.

There they are, the old familiar faces. Neat and smiling, row on row, a lifetime supply. Red or white, who cares. Dry or sweet, who cares. Domestic or imported, who cares. Where, I ask, are the bargains. The bartender knows where they are. And he'll tell. We're in this together.

"First show me your money," he says.

I pull out the piece of paper with the address on it. No. The other pocket. I pull out a five. Picture of what is his name on it. Bald, Father of Confederation. The bartender nods, satisfied.

I point at the bottle of Grateful Red. How much, I ask.

"Five dollars a glass," he says.

I shake my head. Two, I say. That's what it's worth.

He smiles. "To me, maybe. But what's it worth to you?"

This isn't right. Mack'd get me a whole bottle for five. You have anything real cheap, I say. He thinks a minute, reaches down, pulls out a dusty bottle of Burns. At least that's what we call it, because that's what it does. I forget what it is, bourbon maybe. I forget the real name. I haven't seen it in a while, Burns. I think they made it illegal. I'd sooner eat shoe polish, and have, too. But I'm thirsty and I don't have any polish. And Burns is cheap. How much, I say.

"Five," he says with a straight face.

I don't like him. But he's the only friend I have right now.

Burns is a horrible yellow colour, when you shake it you get froth at the top. It tastes sort of like gasoline. The old, leaded kind of gasoline. He starts to put away the bottle.

Wait, I say.

And then they burst in. Three misters with grins as wide as their faces.

"We're celebrating," says the first one. He does a little dance, tap tap tap, stumbles, keeps smiling.

The bartender smiles along with him. "What can I get for you?" he says.

"We've had whisky and gin, and beer and vodka," says the second mister. "Now we want to try something else."

"Not tequila," says the third mister.

They're not quite identical. One of them has a briefcase. But when they struggle up to the bar, the one with the briefcase puts it down, and I can't tell them apart anymore. Glasses, trench coats, wedding rings. How does the song go, rings on their fingers and tassels on their shoes, and they shall have whatever they want.

"How about rum?" says the bartender.

"We've tried it," says the third mister. "What about that stuff there, in the square bottle. What's that?"

"That's Cointreau," says the bartender.

"We'll have Cointreau. Hey you — do you like Cointreau?" the one nearest me asks. He sounds like he's genuinely interested.

I do, I say.

"Will you drink one with us?" he asks.

I will, I say. You'd think we were getting married.

The bartender is happy to pour me a drink he knows he will get paid for. And another. I can't remember the last time a mister bought me anything. Thanks, I tell them. They aren't listening.

"To Revenue Canada!" roars the first one, holding up his glass.

"To audits and their oddities!" says the second.

"May we never have another one!" says the third. I notice he isn't really drinking.

Don't you like it, I ask him quietly.

He frowns. "I've never had it before. It's very orangey, isn't it."

Next thing I know they've gone. The bartender looks up from the cash register.

"You still want that bourbon?" he asks me.

A mostly full glass of Cointreau sits on the bar in front of me. I take it before the bartender can, drink it down, shake my head. And stumble out the door.

There's a big parking garage in the next block. A tall building with cars on every floor. I walk up the ramp. No one looks at me. REMEMBER YOUR SECTION says the sign. I slide into a corner.

Tree-lined streets leading down to the silver lake, ivy-covered walls and small neat front lawns, kids and dogs playing tag through the long afternoons, woods and gardens and delicatessens and the sad faded beauty of a fabled amusement park. It even sounded like a nice place: Sunnyside. Lucy's parents bought us a house there for a wedding present, an odd and ungainly structure on the far side of town — I suppose it was pretty much what they thought of the marriage. After the wedding Arthur went back to work and Lillian went to Italy to recover.

I remember laughing a lot, even at the irritating things that make for funny stories years later. When the armoire wouldn't fit through the bedroom door, when we finally got the hideous wallpaper off and found out it had been hung on top of even more hideous wallpaper, when the basement flooded in the first big storm — actually I wasn't home for the flood, but I laughed when I met the plumber in the front hall late that night. He must have thought I was crazy.

Lucy blamed the house. "The place is cursed!" she said at dinner when the lights went out again without warning. It looked like a bungalow from the front, but it was really a sort of side-back-split — rarely attempted, like one of those jumps the skaters never get quite right. You kept turning corners and finding new rooms. The fuse panel was in the garage. Together we replaced the fuse (I held the flashlight while she rooted around in the dangerous dark) and went back inside. She wanted everything to be perfect. Maybe she thought that I didn't care, but as far as I was concerned things *were* perfect. I loved my work — I'd just been given privileges at the Civic Hospital downtown — and for the first time in my life I loved coming home.

Odd how your sense of home changes. I grew up in three fatherless rooms. For years home meant my mother, obligation, unfulfilled want. Crucifixes and religious mottoes on the walls, *Blessed are the poor for theirs is the Kingdom of Heaven. My reward is in the hereafter.* The efficiency apartment on Manning Avenue was just a place to sleep and study, and bring a girl back if there was no other place to go. And I mean *no* other place — I remember a furtive hand job in the pathology lab, stiff among the stiffs, feeling more comfortable there than in my own room.

Lucy furnished the Sunnyside house herself, went to estate auctions, hung shelving, heaved furniture around. I'd come home and find a beautiful hall-stand in dark oak and marble, hang my coat on it, find it gone the next day. "Too bulky," said Lucy when I asked after it. Or the kitchen table would be white-painted pine on Thursday, huge, squared mahogany on Friday, and round and arborite on Monday. "Which one d'you like?" Lucy would ask, and I had to say I liked them all. I didn't mind what the house looked like. It was enough to come home to Lucy.

I think she enjoyed the control, being able to direct a house instead of just her free time and wardrobe. The funny thing was that a lot of the stuff she bought would have looked just fine at her parents' place. I told her so, meaning it as a compliment, but she was horrified.

"What stuff do you mean?" she cried. We were in the breakfast nook. Yellow wallpaper, adorable miniatures of dogs and chickens, Waterford fruit bowl, a round table this morning, covered in a red gingham tablecloth. "What stuff in particular?"

She seemed to be searching for something of her own, something she could see but not yet reach, beating her wings against the window of her heart's desire. I know she liked being married to me. She liked my being different from her friends' husbands, all of whom worked in their fathers' businesses or not at all. But I don't think marriage was enough for her. Well, why should it be. It wasn't enough for me, even though I loved her more than anyone else, even though she was in a very real sense the anchor of my life. I tried to tell her sometimes, but it always came out wrong. Moira Kilbride's party was a case in point.

I opened the invitation by accident one evening in early summer, after we'd been married a little over a year. Who's Moira Kilbride, I asked. I was sitting by the bedroom window, going through the day's mail. She was in the bathroom doing something to her face.

"A friend," she said. "A new friend, not a close friend, not yet anyway. Why?"

She's invited you and an unnamed escort to go boating with her next Thursday evening, I said.

"Oh good. I was hoping she'd ask me. I met her at the yachting theme party."

What yachting theme party, I asked.

"It was a couple of weeks ago. You weren't there, of course."

I thought of a dozen things to say and discarded them all. Finally I said I would take her to Mrs Kilbride's party.

"That'll be nice, dear." She came out of the bathroom with her hair brushed back and her cheeks scrubbed clean. "The way you took me to the Langtrees' or the Murdochs' or the Arnolds'? Don't you remember how much fun we had at the Oslers'? That was where we all played charades and animal knock." I'd never heard of any of these people before. "Of course, you drank too much claret cup. I remember now, I had to remind you not to eat the cucumber." She went off into peals of laughter.

I was silent, thinking how I'd neglected Lucy, and also, what strange things she and her friends got up to. What's animal knock, I said at length.

"Don't worry, you'll never have to learn it." Her voice, bitter as gratitude, made me wince. "Oh, Mitch, I don't like any of the stupid games, but it would be nice to go to parties together sometimes. Or once. Do you really think you could get to this one? Moira's a lot of fun. You'd like her."

She was pleading with me. I couldn't stand it. Of course I'll go, I said. I'm sorry I've been so busy. You know I'd do anything for you.

She melted perceptibly. "D'you mean it?" I nodded. "You're

sorry. Really sorry. You'll do anything?"

Anything, I said.

"Well then, would you come over here and ... kiss me?"

We kissed. I held her close. Her robe was made of silk, and she wasn't wearing anything underneath. "I was just going to take a shower," she said. "Would you like to join me?"

Would I. My clothes dropped from me like a schoolboy's worries at the sound of the bell. Lucy watched with an amused smile. Turning, she shed her own robe and stalked naked to the bathroom.

A week later, in the breakfast nook, she reminded me of my promise. "You won't forget Mrs Kilbride's party tonight? Pier 14 at six o'clock."

I saluted and said, Aye aye sir. She didn't smile, in fact, she looked kind of bothered. I swallowed a last sip of coffee. I give you my word of honour on it, I said — and could have bit off my tongue because I'd used the exact phrase in connection with another party I'd missed, perhaps the infamous animal knock affair.

Lucy remembered too. "Yes, dear," she said dully. "Now, hadn't you better go? Aren't you late for something?"

And dammit, I was.

The evening was almost a disaster. I worked feverishly all day, skipping a committee meeting and rescheduling my last appointment so I could get my evening clothes from the dry cleaners. I changed in the back of a taxi racing down University

Avenue and — just missed the yacht club ferry. I cursed up and down the waterfront waiting for the next boat, which arrived at the club a matter of moments after Mrs Kilbride's yacht had slipped its mooring. I'd come too far to turn back now. I chartered a launch to catch up to the damn thing — everyone knew which one it was — and loudhailed myself aboard only to find that my wife was not there. She'd phoned her regrets — "Some sort of stomach wog," Mrs Kilbride, a woman the size and shape of Australia, shouted at me through a southwesterly force five of gin and tonic. "Still, now that you're here, let me show you to the bloody bar."

When I got home the first thing Lucy said was, "You're drunk." More in wonder than anger, it seemed to me.

Sherlock bloody Holmes, I muttered.

"It's just that I've never seen you drunk. What happened, did you go to the party? You did, didn't you. I can smell the lake on your tuxedo." She laughed.

What are you so damn cheerful about. I thought you had an upset stomach, I said.

"I don't have an upset stomach. I had one this morning but I feel wonderful now. Wonderful. I just didn't want to go bouncing about Lake Ontario in my condition."

What are you talking about, I said.

"I found out this afternoon. I called your office a dozen times and never got through; I left messages all over the place for you and you never returned them; and it was still the best afternoon of my life. It's official, Mitch. The tests came back positive."

You're pregnant, I said.

She laughed again. She looked wide awake and full of vitamins. Her teeth were so clean it hurt to look at them.

"Dr bloody Watson," she said.

wake up wedged in a concrete corner in the dark, wanting to throw up. So what else is new. Something is rustling and squeaking nearby, maybe rats, maybe bats. I look around for the bottle I was drinking out of, but I can't find it. From the taste at the back of my throat it should be a square, dark bottle. I never liked this stuff. Why anyone would drink it for pleasure I cannot understand. But I am not here on pleasure. I am here on business. Where is the bottle. I feel like what is his name in the story, who smells of rotten apples, only I smell of rotten oranges. Even the thought makes me heave. Am I lying on the bottle. No. The rustling comes from the ceiling. Not rats. Maybe bats.

Time to move. I feel bad and I can't find my bottle, and they're restless overhead. Move before they start to shit on you. Words to live by. I stand up.

Not bats. Pigeons. Guess how I find out.

I move downhill, natural as water. REMEMBER YOUR SECTION say the signs. DO YOU HAVE YOUR CAR KEYS? Cars, pillars, concrete, pigeons. Easy to pick the winner here. LOCK YOUR CAR say the signs. ARE YOUR LIGHTS ON?

A garage for idiots.

No one around. My feet sound bigger than they are. I find

the exit, one of those wooden arm things across it. I duck underneath and walk out to the street. Dark as anything but it's not late any more. It's early. The passing cars look like they just got up. The drivers are drinking coffee. It looks good. Even from where I am on the sidewalk the coffee looks good. It's a little chilly, so I pull my coat around myself this way. When I pull it that way I'm going to sleep.

I'm not tired and I don't have to throw up anymore. I don't recognize this part of Queen Street. A streetcar lumbers by, very slow. On the front is where it's going. CROSSTOWN SUNNYSIDE. The streetcar slows for a red light. I start after it. Hey, wait up, I say. I run — all right, I move as fast as I can, left right left — for maybe half a block. I could go to Sunnyside, I think. I'll see what is his name there, and what is her name, and what is his name. Friends, you understand. I remember their faces. The light stays red. I reach the front doors of the streetcar.

The driver is drinking coffee from a paper cup. I can see the steam. I pound on the doors. Hey, I say. He looks down at me and shakes his head. He thinks I'm asking. The light changes to green. I fumble in my pocket. The streetcar pulls away before I can dig out M. Laurier. I run a while, waving, but it's just exercise. I'm not going to catch the streetcar. Besides, I have to throw up again.

Huge windows full of light and life. A cruise ship, a beach party, the Eiffel Tower. People smiling, waving and why not, everything's half price, romance, excitement, deodorant —

everything. That's inside the store. Outside is a snoring city. The lights change and change again, the signs tell me to walk and I do, and don't walk and I don't. The siren from a distant ambulance fades like a bad dream.

I walk to the end of the block and stop. I know where I am. Graceful white curves stand straight up like celery sticks beside a small round blob of cream cheese. City Hall, where you go skating in the winter. Looks quite festive with the lights shining up on it. Clock chimes in the distance, it's a quarter to something. I walk across the empty square, my footsteps echoing. Someone's sleeping by the what is it, the band shell. Boots and newspapers for warmth. I can hear him snoring. Someone else is leaning forward, wants a fight. Calm down, I tell him. He gives me the old, Oh yeah. I keep walking, try to ignore him.

He hits me. Okay, then.

He's a big guy, much taller than me, and he hits hard, but he's slow. I can tell from the way he shifts his ground that he moves slower than me. I jump around him, but he sticks out his foot and trips me. I get up and kick him hard. Gee, he's in good shape. Doesn't hardly budge. Good muscle tone for a drunk. The guy under the newspaper keeps snoring.

I'm not much of a fighter, started too late, but I've got a few tricks. My best is a head butt to the diaphragm, duck in under the arms and wham, down they go. I've used it a few times. The big guy may be tough as a bootlace knot but his hands are too high. I move in for the head butt.

My head aches even worse than usual when I wake up. It's almost morning, and I'm lying under that bronze statue in front of City Hall. He doesn't look so tough in the light and his hands are still too high, but he's pretty big. No wonder I lost.

I groan. No I don't. I sound different when I groan. It's the drunk with the boots. Sitting up, he's a she. She fumbles around in her clothes, takes out a mickey of something and has a quick swallow. Now I groan. The clock chimes the hour, but I lose count. I use the statue to pull myself up. She sees me. Smiles or snarls, it's hard to tell. She shuffles over. Her boots are too big. "Hi," she says. It's a smile, I guess. Hi, I say.

She holds out the small bottle. It's red inside. "Want some?" she says. Sure, I say. I'm wondering what it is. The bottle looks familiar. I take a swig. Cough syrup. I hate cough syrup. What is his name, Harry, Al, something like that, used to drink it all the time.

"I don't know you, friend," she says. "You get locked out too?" I shake my head, a painful mistake.

"Who are you?" she says. I tell her my name.

"I'm Jill," with that smile that's almost a snarl. "Want some more?" Sure, I say. Not Al or Harry. Constantine. That was the name. Funny, he died of pneumonia.

"I have to pee," says Jill. "And I can't hold it all the way back to the mission." She goes behind the statue. "Don't look," she says. I have to go too. I stay where I am. Where's the mission, I ask. Jill comes out from behind the statue, shaking her hair. It's long and black and straight as the road to hell.

"I'll show you," she says.

richard scrimger

"T his way," says Jill. She leads me behind City Hall, through a gate and onto a curving street with cannons at the end. "It's not far." The sidewalks here are new and clean like bills right out of the bank. There are restaurants with lions in front of them, and stores selling Mountie dolls and maple leaf keychains. We cross the next street without being honked at, Dundas I guess it must be, and even though an arrow tells us to go that way, we go the other way. On my own I always follow the arrow. I figure it knows better than I do. The big street with trees and statues in the middle is University Avenue. That smokestack belongs to Mt Sinai Hospital. I don't feel comfortable. Not that I want to throw up or anything — more uneasy. I'm not used to uneasy. I'm used to throwing up.

"What's the matter?" Jill turns around. She has dark eyes in a dirty face. But I can tell that under the dirt she's probably very pretty. All these hospitals, I say.

"Do you want some more to drink?" She holds out the bottle of cough syrup. I take some. We keep walking. It isn't long before the stores have plucked birds in the windows and baskets of vegetables that aren't carrots or potatoes. Or broccoli. All the signs are in Chinese unless I'm having one of my bad days. She ducks down a side street of locked, frightened buildings. We turn another corner. And another.

"There it is." She points to a big red building, two or three stories high. It's older, set back from the street. The wall is water damaged, the windows have bars on them, the front walk is chipped and cracked. The lawn is mostly mud. Sure looks like home. "And it's open for breakfast," she says.

Someone's sleeping on the steps. He looks like a pile of clothes and he's snoring pretty good. He's got a hat pulled down over his eyes. Nice-looking fur hat.

He hears us coming and sits up, rubbing his eyes, breathing hard. Big strong hands he's got, done a lot of work with them. And a real beard, not a now and again one like mine.

"Hi, friend," Jill says to him.

"I'm no friend of yours."

She doesn't blink. "Want a drink?" She holds out the bottle.

"What's in it?"

"What do you care? It's booze."

He looks over to me. I nod, it's booze all right. I'm starting to feel it. He takes a slug, swallows, frowns at me. "Tastes like shit." As if it was my fault.

I shrug. Better than methanol, I say, and good for your cough too.

"I don't have a cough."

"Not yet, friend." Is Jill talking to herself. She steps between us, takes our arms and walks us up to the big red door. It opens with a push.

"Come on, you two," says Jill. "Hungry?"

Smell of bacon and eggs coming from inside. Bacon and eggs and something else. After a second I recognize the something else. It's cough syrup. And it's coming from me.

Fur hat stops suddenly. He's standing on Jill's boot and it comes off. "You going?" he asks me. I wonder why he cares what I do. I don't care what he does. Jill's hopping around putting on her boot. Her sock is split in the front, I notice. I can see a couple of her toes. "You going?" fur hat asks again.

Why not, I say, it's free.

Inside it's dark and dirty, comforting. There's a wide hallway sloping down, and a narrow staircase going up. We go down. The smell of eggs and bacon and medicine gets stronger. I'm hungry. I remember the last time I ate. No, I don't. Anyway, the food smells good.

The cafeteria is behind a glass door that says UNCONTAMINATED. Who are they kidding. Big steel urns with smilers behind them, steam coming out, a long table covered in elbows and slopped food. All very familiar. Jill pushes me forward. I hold out my plastic plate, get a dump of eggs, another of bacon, toast, a cup of coffee. Jill, behind me, gets the same. It's a quiet place. People stare vacantly into their eggs, into their spilled coffee, into their puddle of drool. They sniff and wipe their mouths and don't notice us at all.

Hello everyone, I say, sitting down, being polite, how are

you doing. They stare like old potatoes, all eyes. Jill shushes me. I shrug and get eating. The table's crooked and there's a dribbler uphill from me. That's too bad. But the food's okay.

A guy down at the end pulls a bottle of cough syrup from his coat. He takes a drink, puts it back. No one stops him. I wait for a smiler to swoop down and take it away, but no. Jill pours some syrup into my coffee. I stare at her. She winks. I open my mouth to say something. She shakes her head, puts the bottle away. I wonder where it all comes from. My coffee tastes horrible. I drink some more.

I'm feeling woozy. The room is spinning very slowly. Urns, tables, steam, silence, then the urns again. I take a big sip of coffee, push my chair away from the table and relax into it.

I can't find the back of the chair. There it is. No, that's the floor. It feels soft and warm.

wake up feeling lousy. I have a headache like a grand piano between the eyes and someone is pounding out a polka. Mind you, I'm not cold or hungry, mustn't complain. I don't know how it happens, but I'm sitting up and there's a pen in my hand. I mean, I've woken up holding some weird things but — a pen.

"*Sign here.*" Here is a sheet of paper. A form with a lot of writing and a space for my name. My chair is orange. It doesn't fit me. I don't think it would fit anyone. What's going on. I try to read the form. "*Sign your name.*" The Voice of Authority. The same voice that tells me to *Move along*, to *Put it back on the shelf*, to *Get out of here*. What can I do. A word pops out at me from the form. Experiment. Wait a minute, I say. But I've already signed.

"Welcome to the Pharm Trex Faith and Charity Mission," says the Voice. "Take him down, nurse." I reach for the paper but it's gone. The world turns around, no, it's my chair that's moving. I try to get out but I'm wearing a safety belt.

"There there, now. We don't want to make a fuss, do we." A nurse. No one else talks like that. Actually, I do want to make a fuss, but I'm tired and I feel like something the dog wouldn't eat. "Just relax, sir. We'll be downstairs in a minute and you can have a nice rest."

That shuts me up. Haven't been called sir in years.

The elevator feels as old as I do, moves down very slowly as if it doesn't trust itself, then gives a sigh of relief when we get off. There are two sets of doors that swish open and shut, and a smell of soap and blood and the kind of alcohol you shouldn't drink. Very familiar. The doctor's office is big and dirty, just like him. He's leaning against the desk. His pants ride up around his stomach and he's showing a lot of white meat above his sock. Drab greasy hair hangs in his eyes. Not exactly Rex Morgan.

"Hi, beautiful," he says to the nurse, cracking his gloved knuckles with a sound like the school bully eating your apple. "This one's awake," he says. All those years in medical school. "Well, I guess it doesn't matter." He takes a syringe from a covered tray, squeezes out a drop of something. Hey, I say.

I have a bad feeling. Rex is being very careful with the needle. Like he's going to inject me with poison or something. Is this the experiment.

"There there." Rex smiles nervously and moves towards me, holding the needle in front of him. "There there." The nurse pats my shoulder. She's wearing gloves too. Rex takes a step closer and I kick him right in the morgans. Don't mean to, I was aiming for the needle, but it works just as well. He doubles over and the needle goes flying. I can't undo the safety belt, damn. I shove back with both feet and knock over the nurse. I'm yelling for help and so is she, funny how we both want the same thing, but she gets it and I don't. More white coats. I thresh around for a bit and then my chair falls over and my arm stops working. I'm on the floor, caught like a salmon in a net. And here comes the gaff.

I wake up in bed with my hand in a frilly bandage like a drumstick in a classy restaurant. Which makes me a turkey. Someone nearby is coughing. Hard to say what time it is. Not that I care a lot. I'm hungry and I feel sick. Do I want to eat first and then throw up, or throw up right away. I notice a Band-Aid on the inside of my elbow. Right over the vein. Sonofabitch, I say.

"Hello, Mitchell." It's the Voice of Authority again. Turns out to belong to a craggy, handsome man with a long chin and long hair and deep grooves in his forehead from worry. Long gloved fingers. "My name is Dr Royal and I want to know," he pauses like an actor selling soap, "how you're feeling." I throw up at him, missing, of course, most of it lands on me. He glides away. "Orderly!"

I'm ready to sleep. I'm ready to cry. I'm ready to take a drink. Boy, am I ready to take a drink. The guy in the next bed is familiar. It's what is his name from breakfast, with the fur cap. He looks sad.

Hi, I say. What's your name.

Slowly, slowly, like traffic crawling past a messy accident, his face clears. "Hello, Mitchell," he says. His voice is hoarse, deep. His name is Joe.

What happens now, Joe, I ask him. When are they going to

kick us out.

"I don't think they're going to kick us out," he says.

Then how are we going to get something to drink, I say.

He smiles, not very happily. "Everyone has something to drink here," he says. He points to the table beside my bed. Sure enough, there's a bottle on it. Cough syrup. "You're supposed to drink. That's what they told me when I got my shots. Stay as long as you can, they said. And drink as much as you want."

You don't you have any — whisky on you, Joe, I say. Or cheap red, or anything.

He shakes his head.

Someone a few beds over coughs. It's like a signal, everyone joins in. Nice variety of tone, from the surprised soprano hack right down to the real rumblebelly. We could be in an opera, the famous coughing chorus from *I Tuberculosi*.

Joe takes a swig from his bottle of medicine. "They say this stuff'll makes you better," he tells me.

Better than what, I want to know. An orderly comes by with a mop and bucket. He's wearing a mask. I feel a tickle at the back of my throat. I reach for my bottle. Let's get out of here, I say to Joe. You and me, we'll go get ourselves a real bottle. What about it.

He turns back and laughs. I think he laughs. His mouth is open anyway, and he's saying ha ha ha. I guess he's laughing.

I take a drink. You know, the stuff isn't as bad as all that. I start to cough.

richard scrimger

t's my first night in the new place and I'm feeling a little low. My hand hurts so much I can't sleep. Across the room Spawn of Satan is having a nightmare and Luis, I think that's his name, is coughing. The room's full of blood and vomit, pretty much like any other place I've stayed. There's a little tickle at the back of my mind where I can't reach it. My throat tickles too, but I know what to do about that. I lean over to get my bottle of cough syrup. They call it elixir here, Joe told me. Whatever. I reach for the bottle, only I forget about my bandage. I can't hold on and the bottle falls onto the floor. It breaks. I hear it break. It breaks and all the cough syrup is gone.

I'd call for help, but who would hear me over the racket of the nightmare and the coughing. I lie awake thinking about a place where they feed you and then give you a needle and a place to sleep it off, and somehow you end up with a sore throat.

A name swims sluggishly into my brain, like a fish through ice-thick water. Pharm Trex. A familiar name. Not a car or a running shoe. More of an antibiotic, coagulant, wart remover name. Shelves full of jars, drawers full of Blue Cross stickers and credit card receipts — that kind of name. Pharm Trex. Where do I know it from. And why does it make me want to cry.

Breakfast is after a bell. We troop down the hall like schoolkids, me and Joe and Spawn of Satan and a couple of dribblers. Luis is too sick to go. His sheets are red where he's been coughing.

Same food as yesterday, steamed eggs and toast, but a different room. The sign on the door says CONTAMINATED. The smilers are wearing masks, so you can't tell if they're smiling or not. The tables are crowded and it's a lot noisier. Coughing mostly. Joe and I sit together. He shares his bottle of syrup. I'm not used to eating so regularly. Three meals yesterday, and here's another one. I eat but I'm not really hungry.

From a few tables over I hear, "Spawn of Satan!" He's a cross-eyed pint-pot of a guy with a voice like a barrel. He doesn't talk unless you ask him something, and then that's all he ever says. Maybe someone asked him to pass the salt.

There's a guy with a skull wrap at our table. What happened to you, I ask him. He stares. Were you trying to escape, I say, showing him my bandaged hand. Escape, you know, run away. I got hurt trying to run away, I say.

His eyes get real wide and he says, "Lrrr." That's all. "Lrrr." So much for him. I drink some coffee. It doesn't taste bad with cough syrup. Maybe I'm getting used to it.

From another table I hear raised voices. "What about the Prime Minister?" Political discussion, I'm surprised.

"He's the Spawn of Satan!"

"And the mayor?"

"Spawn of Satan!"

"And Ronald McDonald?"

The woman next to me is sweating. "I'm going back to bed. I don't feel too good." She sways towards the door. Eggs do that to me too, sometimes. A smiler swoops down to clear the half-empty plate. Hang on, I say, helping myself to the old woman's toast. It's done the way I like it, kissed by the toaster. That's my mom's phrase. I remember Roscoe laughing when I used it on a waitress. "Not me, sister, I want mine buggered, beaten and left for dead by the toaster," he said with a leer. The girl practically gagged.

Great bronchial spasm across from me. Long slug from the bottle of cough syrup. The skull wrap says, "Lrrr." A smiler comes round, clears away my plate and coffee cup. Doesn't take the bottle of cough syrup. Thanks, I say. She smiles, I think, and goes away.

The tubs of food are gone and hoses are turned on the tables. Breakfast is over. We're all moving to the doors. Joe is somewhere up ahead. I'm beside the guy with the skull bandage. What happens now, I say. He doesn't answer. He's having a little trouble getting around the tables.

This is my first morning, I tell him. Do we get to go outside. I could use some fresh air. How about you. Unless it's raining. I hate rain, don't you, I say. I know you don't have to shovel rain, but, let's face it, guys like us don't have to shovel snow either.

He trips over a chair. Careful, I say. I help him up. What's your favourite thing to do, I ask. If you could do anything right now, what would it be. He looks at me.

"Lrrr," he says. He nods.

I nod back. Me too, I say.

Pregnancy was the best thing that ever happened to Lucy. As her stomach grew and rounded, so did her confidence, as if she'd been born too light and needed the extra weight. I'd seen this phenomenon before — "big" with child seems to be a condition of the personality as much as the body — but never to such a marked degree. Lucy smiled the whole day long, from breakfast to bedtime. She did exercises, ate sensibly, decorated the nursery, balanced her chequebook, took classes at the Art College. "Good on you, mate!" said Moira Kilbride. She and Lucy had become great friends. Moira encouraged her in everything, even the outsized metal sculpture. "Good on you! Four months preggers and welding up a storm. Bloody good!" Lucy looked so enthusiastic, reporting this to me, that I couldn't say anything except, That's great. For one thing, it was midnight and I was just getting in the door. Lucy, still awake, with dirt under her fingernails and a smile on her face, had more energy than I did.

I'll never forget the first time the baby moved. We were at her parents on one of my rare Sunday afternoons off. Arthur and Lillian and the oak-panelled, tapestried dining-room, steak-

and-kidney pie dished out by Grover the butler, who still called me "sir" instead of my name, and suddenly amid the quiet of properly handled cutlery a murmur of surprise and delight.

"Lucy, dear, if you have something to say perhaps you'd like to tell all of us." I think she expected to upset her daughter. Lillian was not a kind person. Between the two of us was a poorly kept truce; between her and Lucy was something else.

Now, Lillian, I said — I used her first name whenever I could, searching for the flicker in her eyes that told me a shot had landed — you sound like a school teacher telling little Johnny to share his joke with the class. I smiled across the table, but Lucy didn't need any support at all.

"I wasn't talking to you, mother," she said. "I wasn't talking to any of you."

"Then I suppose you were talking to yourself. Not a particularly refined habit, dear."

Habits, I began, are like sugars: the refined ones aren't necessarily the best for you. At the far end of the table Arthur snickered and then cleared his throat. There was hope for Arthur, he was starting to unbend a bit. Lillian shot him a look.

"There, she's gone back to sleep," said Lucy. "Night night, sweetheart."

"Let me take your plate, sir." I hadn't finished, but Lillian ran a tight ship, lunch was served at 12:30 and over at 1:30. Have you ever thought, I'd asked once, of installing half-hour bells. I was about to fight Grover for my lunch when the significance of Lucy's last remark hit me. Is the baby moving, I asked her. It's only the eighteenth week.

She nodded. Eighteen weeks is early, I said. We might have a genius here — or a gymnast. Lucy smiled.

"If it's a girl, I'm going to call it Cheryl Ann," she said.

"That's a name without very much distinction," said Lillian. "Perhaps we'd better hope for a boy." She smiled at her daughter. Six months earlier Lucy might have gasped and begun to cry. That day she smiled right back.

"Fuck off, mom," she said. Grover dropped my plate on the floor. Arthur opened his mouth so wide a small piece of steak-and-kidney pie fell out. The next day half a ton of scrap iron arrived at the house and Magda Opara's test results came back.

The sonogram confirmed my suspicions. Magda was twenty-five weeks pregnant. I called her father at once. She'll have to stay in the hospital at least two days, I said. There's a greater chance of complication when she's this far along.

"I see. No chance of ... of the ... " He couldn't say it. I knew what he was asking.

Almost none, I said. A twenty-five-week-old fetus is not viable. Will you tell your daughter, I asked, or would you like me to.

"No need to trouble her about this," he said. "Risks, complications, it'll only worry her unnecessarily. You can tell her afterwards about staying the extra day in hospital. Tell her when it's over — that's the best way with Magda."

"Oh." And that was that. I didn't think much more about it then because something came up — Mrs Volkof with twins, I think. That's the great thing about being a doctor. Something always comes up.

"How awful for her," said Lucy that night when I told her a bit about the case. No last names, just Magda and Leon. "How awful for her. Poor girl." Not exactly poor, I said.

"What are you going to do?" She was sitting up in bed, wearing a frilly nightie that looked dumb and strangely sexy at the same time.

I was brushing my teeth. Do about what, I said.

"About the baby. Now that you know it's got a real chance of survival."

Hold on a minute, I said. The baby is not my patient, Magda is. And it's not a baby yet, it's a fetus the size of a mouse and its chance of survival is still almost nonexistent.

"It's as far along as ours, isn't it? The fetus?"

A little farther, actually, I said.

"What if it was another month older?"

I spat, rinsed, frowned into the mirror at a pimple. If it was a month older, I said, it'd have a much better chance. But what's the point of that kind of speculation; if it was three months older it'd be almost full term.

"So the baby — sorry, the fetus — is probably moving inside her. What can she be thinking right now."

I slid into bed. She's not thinking anything, I said. She's hoping the whole problem will go away. That's usually the case, I said. The number of dumb, apathetic, cow-daughters I'd seen in my office, nodding, Yes dad, Yes mom, whatever you say, chewing their gum, Yes doctor, letting themselves be herded down the hall for their injections.

Lucy reached for the top button of my pyjamas. "Did you tell her?" She undid the button and slid her hand inside. Her fingers rippled across my chest, emerging to undo another button. And another. Tell her what, I said. Lucy's frilly nightie came with a drawstring bow at the front. I pulled the string and flung open the pink lacy gathers. We settled back against the pillows. "Did you tell her," Lucy leaned forward to lick the hollow at the base of my throat, then trailed her tongue down to my nipple. She took it in her mouth, sucking dreamily for a moment, "how close she was to being a mother?" We kissed, and I tasted salt on her tongue. I told her father, I said.

Lucy's breasts stuck out proud and firm, like little white kaiser helmets from the First World War. I polished them with my palms, gently working towards the sensitive pink spike at the top. She shivered. "Don't you think," she said, pulling my head down, "that she should have a chance to reconsider?" My mouth closed over one nipple, my hand over the other. I tugged gently with my teeth. "Oh my." That was her; I was too busy to answer. "Oh my, yes." Lucy's fundus came up to just below her navel. There was a lovely fullness about her lower abdomen. I gave a final pretend bite to her aureole and moved down her belly.

I ... think, I said, speaking between kisses, she ... knows ... what ... she ... wants. By now I was at the edge of the pubic forest which spread, dense and curling, down to the lush and fertile valley where civilization begins. Lucy groaned and moved herself down the bed. I followed, exploring delicately, fingers blazing the trail for my lips and tongue.

"Then why did she wait so long to approach you?" Lucy had difficulty with my pyjama bottoms. I had to help her get them off, not that I minded. We lay like ships moored bow to stern for cargo transfer. My erect penis shuddered near her mouth. She clutched it in her hand and licked the tip, a hot strawberry ice cream cone. I don't know, I said. I was having trouble concentrating. "Tell her," said Lucy before taking another, longer lick. She rolled me onto my back and climbed over me. Legs spread, she hunkered down so that her vulva opened in my face like a stormy night. I reached up to lick a raindrop. "She should know all the facts before deciding." I mumbled something. "Don't stop," said Lucy. I kept mumbling. She sat down hard, arching her back, so that her pubic bone mashed into my mouth. My tongue kept jiggling against her clitoris. She rubbed herself back and forth on my face, like a bear on a scratching post. I couldn't hear or see. My world was wet and dark, slippery and aromatic. She rubbed faster and faster, then slowed, prolonging each contact. She began to tremble. I reached up and she grabbed my searching hands and held them to her breasts, squeezing hard. Her nipples felt like cigars between my fingers. Suddenly she went into spasm, bucking against my mouth, against my outthrust tongue, time and again, hard enough to hurt. I felt like the saddle on a rodeo bull. Then the rains came, drenching my cheeks and chin. Her movements slowed, softened, and after a moment she slid off me. Still on her knees, she bent her head to smile. Her face was wet with perspiration and she was flushed down to the tops of her breasts. "That was great," she said. "I just love coming all over your face." I like it too, I said.

She stroked the gentle rise and fall of my chest and stomach down to the sudden outcrop of bare anatomy between my legs. "And are you going to see your patient again to tell her about the baby?" She reached down to cup my balls. I moved my legs to make it easier for her. She knows about the baby, I said. That's why she asked for an abortion. I don't see what I could tell her to change her mind, I said. Lucy slipped a finger down to tickle my anus.

"You could tell her she'll regret her choice," she said, bending over to bestow a chaste kiss to the base of my erection. Her lips worked their way up the underside of the shaft, barely touching the skin. It was like getting a wing job from a butterfly.

She may regret the choice, I said, grimacing, but it's hers to make. It's her body.

Lucy didn't say anything for a moment. Her breathing slowed. She was getting excited again. How do they do that. When I come back to earth I want to be a woman. We sat up together and kissed. She stuck a finger in our mouths and then used it to play with herself. Her heart rate increased. I could feel it. When we pulled apart her eyes were glazed over. She flopped down on her pillow with her ass high in the air, a position she often chose for masturbation. Her hand snaked between her legs to fondle herself. I watched closely. First she rubbed herself all over with her fingertips, the way you rub garlic into a leg of lamb. Then she pulled open her inner lips to stick a whole finger inside. After a moment the finger withdrew and then crooked beckoningly at me. Well, I never needed an engraved invitation. I scrambled over on my knees and entered the door she held open for me. Time stood still. Space stretched out as warm and inviting as a crescent roll fresh from the oven. "Oh, wow," she said, unless it was me. How do you know, I said, that she'll regret her choice. Not all women do.

"I know because I did," she told me, writhing, thrusting her buttocks back into me. "I had an abortion when I was seventeen and I've regretted it ever since. Come on now, harder. Harder." But I couldn't because, suddenly, I wasn't. Time zoomed past me, space curved and so did I, just like a, well, a crescent roll. Really, I said. How did you ... I mean, who decided ... I didn't know how to put it. I grabbed her soft rounded ass, trying to recapture the moment.

"My mom did all the planning. I went to the hospital overnight, and no one talked about it afterwards." She squeezed with her pelvic muscles. I felt like a piece of Play-Doh. It had never occurred to me to ask about her medical past. Of course her mom had done all the planning. "Getting pregnant was a mistake," Lucy went on. "I didn't want to have a baby, I wasn't in love. I should have known better and so should the boy I was with. I hardly remember him at all. But I often think about the — the fetus. I never saw it, you know. The doctor said it was better that way, but I wish I'd been able to say goodbye." She pushed back against me, gripping hard.

"Come on now, Mitch," she crooned. "Squeeze my ass. You know I love that. Squeeze it hard. That's it. Now reach underneath and rub my tits. Can you do that. Feel how hard they are? My nipples are standing straight out. Twist them. Oh yes. Harder. Pinch them. Oh my, yes." I began, slowly, to reconsider my position. Maybe I'd been wrong about Magda. Yes. She should have all the facts before making her choice. Lucy kept encouraging me and as she talked I could feel my resolve getting harder and harder.

"Oh my. What a cock you have, Mitch. You feel so good inside me, hard and big, God, you're like a cannon." I decided to speak to Magda the very next day. "Come on, Mitch, come on, fire that cannon into me, fire your salute, fire one, fire two, oh yes, keep firing, I want twenty-one guns, come on, Mitch, make me a queen!"

Opara insisted on being present when I talked to his daughter. I couldn't very well refuse. "Doctor Mitchell just wants to make sure you know your own mind on this, Magda," he said, when we were all sitting down in my office. It was Monday morning and wet outside. The bottom of Magda's honey-coloured haircut was fringed and darker than the rest. I tried to see inside her, tried to imagine what she was feeling. She gave me no help. Rain-damped hair aside, she might have been a mannequin.

You know, Magda, that the test you did — the sonogram — showed you to be almost six months pregnant, I said. No

richard scrimger

reaction. Magda, that lump of tissue we're going to force out of you tomorrow is already moving. How do you feel about that, I said. You've carried it for six months. In another three you'll have a healthy baby. Did you ever think of the alternatives to abortion: keeping the baby, or carrying to term and putting him up for adoption.

Leon Opara was staring at me. I couldn't tell if he was angry or not. His daughter looked like she'd gone into a trance. She stared at me, unblinking. "A baby," she whispered, "A baby." As if she'd never thought about what was going on inside her until this moment.

"Goddammit," said Opara.

"And it's already alive?"

I nodded. I saw it move on the sonogram, I said. Kicking and turning over. Can't you feel it kicking, Magda, I said.

She had this little smile on her face. "A baby," she repeated. "I'm going to kill a baby."

We stared at her. "Magda." Opara was so shocked he actually sounded like he cared for her. "Little muffin. You don't mean that. You can't mean that. Here. Hold your father's hand."

Her eyes were full of hate. "You say it's alive? There's something alive in here? Doing this to me?" She gestured down at her swollen body. "Making me sick? Giving me headaches and rashes and piles?" She tapped her stomach sharply, the way you tap someone to make sure they're paying attention. It was a macabre gesture. I nodded.

"Well, doctor, if it lives, show it to me. I want the little bastard to squirm."

I tried to hide my dismay. Squirming, I said, is probably what it'll do best.

My hand itches. I know that's good, everything healing inside, but so what. It itches like the seven Furies, even the fingers sticking out of the bandage. I rub them in my hair. It doesn't help much. Joe says his leg itches. I figure he's got vermin. I mean, my leg itches too, but not like my hand.

Our beds are still side by side. We talk at night when I can't sleep because of my cough. We talk about ourselves. He tells me about growing up in the old country, sounds horrible, a desert with no prospects. What about school, I ask him, and he shakes his head. He learned to read and write and that's about all.

"I envy you, Mitch," he says one night. "You had opportunities."

And a mother to make sure they didn't go to waste, I say. Don't forget that. After dad died my mother worked her fingers to the bone at the IGA to put me through school, and every night she'd come home and show me the bones. For you, she'd tell me, I'm doing it all for you, so study hard, go to mass, be good, think of me all the time. She brought home dented cans and rotten vegetables from the store for dinner, meat the inspectors hadn't passed and day-old bread. She begged clothes from neighbours. She prayed aloud for my success every night.

Do you know what it's like living under that kind of obligation, I say. You've got to be fucking perfect.

"It's tough, I know." How does he know, I wonder.

Go to school, be a doctor, she told me, be a success and be eternally grateful, never stop, it's what you owe me for killing myself for you. That was my mom. I hated everything about her, I say. I'm surprised at myself, my hands are shaking.

"I always honoured my mother," he says stoutly. Uh huh, I say.

"I did."

So you ran away with your wife, I say, because you honoured your mother.

"That was different. That was life and death. I was worried about the baby."

Which your mother had never seen, I say. So the three of you left the country without telling anyone. Your mom never saw the child. She didn't even know if it was a boy or a girl. Face it, Joe, I say, we're a lot alike.

I have to cough. By the way, was the baby a boy or a girl, I ask.

"A boy." He turns his head away, doesn't say any more. Memories are tough when you're in a strange place in the dark and someone nearby is shouting "Spawn of Satan" every few minutes.

Mornings we see Dr Royal. He listens to our chests, looks in our mouths, sighs and tosses his head to get the hair out of his eyes. Sometimes he has a nurse with him. She says, Yes doctor and melts when he looks at her. Other times he has a couple of orderlies with him. They don't say anything, not even when they drop a body. I remember the dribbler's head landing on the floor with a sound like a clean single to right field — didn't matter to him by then, but the rest of us felt it. After our checkup, promise you won't laugh, some of us go to the exercise room. The others stay in their beds and cough. The first few days I ask if I can go outside and the doctor says not yet. After a while I stop asking.

I like the exercise room because it has windows. We go up the back stairs through more doors marked CONTAMINATED. I wonder if we should wear bells like lepers, or do I mean jesters. The glass is thick and dirty but you can see through the bars. One day a convertible goes by with the top down, makes me think. What time is it, I ask Joe.

"10:30," he says. Don't ask me how, but Joe always knows what time it is.

No no, I say, what time of year. One of the orderlies tells us to get into a line. I cough.

"It's summer," says Joe. We're standing close to the window. Sure looks like summer, leaves on the trees, shorts on the kids, yellow monsters digging up the streets. No wonder I'm so hot, I say.

The orderly tells us to touch our heads and shoulders knees and toes. Most of us aren't paying attention. He has to start again.

"It's not that hot," says Joe. He's still wearing his hat. "Not like in the old country."

Heads and shoulders knees and toes, knees and toes, knees and — Joe and I bend together, I cough a lot of blood all over his — toes.

I stare at it. That's my sickness. Joe stares too. Then he sighs and wipes it away with his hand. Careful, I say, that's dangerous.

"I know," he says.

You'll get my sickness, I say.

"I know," he says.

Sausages for lunch. Joe doesn't eat sausages. "It's hard to get over being born Jewish," he explains. At the next table someone is in convulsions. Smilers are dragging him away from the table. Everyone else is too busy chewing or coughing to notice. Pretty hard to get over being born at all, I say, reaching for Joe's helping.

Sometimes we go for walks in the afternoon. That means down the hall to the glass doors and back. Not exactly scenic unless you like drains and concrete. I keep expecting to bump into "Lrrr" again but I don't. The closest I come is a woman in a neck brace clutching a handful of leftover sausages. Not very close, I guess, but she has the same eyes as "Lrrr."

I start to feel better, go longer and longer without coughing. Soon it's a whole day. Then I can't remember when I coughed last. Not Joe, he gets worse and worse. Lungs like a Texas oil field, only it's not oil he's coughing up. He can't go to exercises, and after a while he doesn't even come to the cafeteria. I bring food to our room but he won't eat that either.

Dr Royal shows a lot more interest in me after I stop being sick. I think I make a pleasant change for him. We go for X-rays — I have them, he just watches. We had a long session yesterday. Today he looks like a man with a winning lottery ticket.

"How's our star patient," he says to me.

I'm fine, I say. He smiles broadly, makes a note on his clipboard. Why don't you look at my friend, I say, he's got a bad cough.

"We know about Joe," the doctor says. "We're more interested in you." But I don't have a cough, I say.

"Yes." His eyes blaze like hot coals.

After lunch we have a visitor from outer space. That's what she looks like, she's wearing a special suit from a sterile ward. Dr Royal shows her around, points us out like items of interest on her goodwill tour from Mars. He stops in front of my bed.

"This is the subject I told you about," he says.

"Ah, yes." Her voice is filtered. "*He's* the one." I smile and wave. She looks past me at the doctor. "You're sure you've got his consent form," she says. "Pharm Trex doesn't want any trouble with the government."

"Quite sure," says Dr Royal.

I'm awake when they come for me that night. Joe and I are talking about religion. "I just can't believe you were ever a serious Christian," he says.

You're right, I tell him. It wasn't me, it was my mom all along. But I was a serious non-Christian, I say. When I left the church I locked the door after me and threw away the key. He laughs until he starts to cough.

That's when the three orderlies come. They're wearing rubber aprons and one of them carries shampoo and a razor, so I figure they're the lice police, we had them at St Pete's too. But they don't go near the new guy across the room, hair down to there and you can see things crawling in it, great big things. They don't worry about Joe and his fur cap. They come straight to my bed and before I know it I'm down the hall in the shower. Three people to clean and shave me, I might be royalty. I can wash myself, I say, and they don't listen. Hey, that hurts, I say, and they don't listen. My hair parts on the left, I say, and they don't listen. Did Louis XIV have this problem.

"There now, ain't he a picture," says one. He has his head on one side, admiring. Another one is putting me into hospital pyjamas. The third is sweeping up.

I look in the mirror and gasp. Dark eyes in a dead white face and no hair. I'm a skull. It can't be me, but there's no one else in the room with these three guys. I touch my smooth head, so does the guy in the mirror. I pick my nose, so does he. Sonofabitch.

"Who's that?" whispers what is his name from a nearby bed. He's new.

"Is that you, Mitch?" Joe sounds surprised.

"It's the Spawn of Satan!" from across the room.

Hi guys, I say.

"You look like a ghoul," says Joe.

"He's the Spawn of Satan I tell you!"

I know I shouldn't let this worry me. Come on, Joe. It's me, I say.

"Where's your bandage? Mitch had a bandage on his hand. You don't."

They took it off in the shower, I say. The orderlies gave me a shower and took off my bandage. Hurt like hell too, I say. See, here's the mark.

"Spawn of Satan for sure!"

Joe looks right at me. "I wonder," he says, and starts to cough.

I take a sip of cough syrup and lie back.

Next morning Joe doesn't get up with the bell. Did I mention there was a bell. Not the trumpet thing for the army, what's it called, Rivoli, no, ravioli. Not that, just a school bell, I wake up each morning thinking I'm late for Latin class.

Joe, Joe, I say, bending over him. He isn't moving. He looks pretty bad. Then his eyes flicker. You okay, Joe, I say. He turns his head and coughs. Yuck. But he's awake.

"Who are you?" he whispers. I tell him.

"Oh yes, I remember now." His eyes jerk open. "I had a dream about you," he says. "They took you downstairs and poisoned you."

He's got a lot of energy all of a sudden, sitting up in bed, it can't be good for him. No no, I say. Don't worry, they just gave me a shower. Lie down now, Joe. Can I bring you something, I say. Cup of coffee, piece of toast. I stop talking when he grabs hold of me.

"They sacrificed you like a lamb. Your blood was clean and they poisoned it."

They shaved my head, I say. And gave me pyjamas.

"You're in danger, Mitch. This place is a big laboratory and we're the rats." He falls back, breathing fast and light, too exhausted to cough.

I straighten him out, pat his hand. Poor guy, he may be right at that. But the rats don't get to leave the laboratory, do they. And it's breakfast time — only it turns out it isn't. Dr Royal is early today. His eyes gleam when he sees me.

"Ah, Mitchell, there you are. You're clean and shaved. Good. No dirty bandage, no head lice." Not much you can say to that.

"Don't go to the cafeteria, Mitchell, you're not supposed to have any food." The doctor stands in the doorway rubbing his hands briskly. "I'll see you in a couple of hours. Have some cough syrup if you like, but nothing else." He vanishes.

Joe tries to lift his head again but he's too tired. Or maybe the fur hat's too big. He looks really bad. I ask is there anything I can do for him. He smiles like I've said something funny.

"Think of me at ... ten o'clock." His voice is faint. He coughs without moving his chest and a small trickle of blood comes out of his mouth.

Okay, I say. No point in telling him I don't have a watch. My stomach rolls, funny how you get used to three meals a day.

After a while his lips move, but I can't hear what he says. I bend right down. "I'll see you later," he whispers.

Why, where are you going, I say. He doesn't answer. I guess I know where he's going.

Thunder outside. Sounds like quite a storm. The lights flicker. I stare at Joe. What's it like, I ask. Are you still there, Joe, can you tell me.

He hears me, mouths my name. His smile flickers on and

off like the lights.

"It doesn't ... hurt, Mitch," he says. When he swallows his throat looks all scaly. "This is not the worst thing that's ever happened to me."

What could be worse, I wonder. He hears me. Thunder again. The building shakes. Joe's eyes are wide open and full of tears. He squeezes my hand. "Losing my son," he says in a choked voice. "That's the worst thing. Isn't it, Mitch. You know, don't you. Oh, Jesus."

I don't know what to say. I'll see you later, I tell him, but for him it's already later.

The orderlies strap me into a chair and wheel me away. Different corridor than last time but the same orderlies, same style of conversation. Where are we going, I ask, and they don't answer. Why does the door say TOXIC CODE THREE DANGER, I ask, and they don't answer, but we stop so they can put on masks. Don't I get a mask, I say, and they don't answer. They push me into an air lock. At the other end is a nurse in a space suit. She jabs me under the neck with a needle and hooks me up to a drip feed. Then she rolls me over to Dr Royal. He's dressed for the moon too.

"Hello again, Mitchell," he says jovially. "Ready to make history?" Meaning what, have I written out a will. The room is small and so white it hurts my eyes.

Don't I get a suit, I ask. The doctor laughs.

"You won't need one," he says. There's a microphone

inside his helmet. His voice sounds tinny and distant, and I can hear his breathing. "It's September 28th," he says, "and almost exactly 09:40 hours." Thanks, I tell him, what's the weather like, but he's not talking to me now. He goes on. "Bearing in mind the reaction of our last candidate, I have placed Mitchell on a sodium pentathol drip — damn." The lights flicker and go out. "Nurse! Find out what's going on."

I'm hungry and tired. My stomach growls sleepily. It's tired too. Maybe I do go to sleep, because the next thing I know I'm on a rolling bed, a gurney. The doctor is bending over me. He's still got that smile. I want to wipe it off, only I can't because my arms are strapped down. And my legs. I guess I'm going to let the doctor get away with it for now.

He's talking into the microphone again. "It's 10:00 and candidate Mitchell is now fully relaxed," he says. "I'm removing the infected sample from storage and preparing to administer the injection."

I know I should be worried, but I can't seem to work myself up. Not about me anyway. I'm sad about Joe. Tears come to my eyes. The nurse and doctor are bending over me in their silly suits. The nurse says, "Don't worry. You're doing great." Sounds like Jane Ford, no Honda, one of those car companies. Fuck off, I say. "That's right. Good for you." I guess she can't understand me. The doctor flicks the end of the syringe to clear it, and looks at my neck where the drip feed is going in. His face is hungry — Dracula looks at necks that way.

The syringe descends, halting at the sound of the what is it, we used to get them all the time at St Pete's. Fire alarm, that's it.

Blinding, choking clouds of smoke. My lungs are full. My eyes ache. I feel sick. It sure is exciting. My mouth is dry as ashes. I wish we could move faster. I'm still strapped to the gurney, all I see is smoke and bits of the ceiling flashing by, and the doctor and nurse running hard. But I can hear it nearby, growling, licking at the walls like a bear after honeycomb. Fire.

"Quick! Where's the emergency exit?" gasps the doctor. He's dressed like a doctor now, not an astronaut. The nurse points. We take the turn quickly and the gurney bumps against the far wall. She smiles down at me reassuringly. They train them well, nurses. Off the gurney, wrapped in a sheet. They carry me up the stairs together.

The first door we try is blocked, so we climb some more. There's a lot of smoke when we get into the upstairs hallway. Paint is bubbling on the walls. "Cover your mouth," the doctor says. "His too." She pulls the sheet higher. Flannel in my mouth. I'm surprised at the concern for my health — grateful but surprised. "We'll try through here," says the doctor and then, "Damn! That door is hot!"

"Hello! Hello!" calls a new voice from a long way away. "Anyone left in there! Answer me, if you can, before I turn all crispy!"

"Over here!" call the doctor and nurse together. "We're over here!"

"Keep shouting! Where are you?" An accent like someone I used to know at St Pete's, a sad drinker, what was his name.

"The second floor!" calls the doctor. "By the east stairs." He chokes. Even through the sheet I can taste smoke and death and fear. Reminds me of the pastrami place near the barracks at Queen and Jarvis.

"Don't go down! The ground floor is gone. I'm ahead of you. Move towards my voice, if the sound of it doesn't offend you!" Sad Tim was his name, at least that's what we called him, Sad Tim from Antrim. "And keep talking, or else it's not conversation."

They drag me down the hall, not fast enough. "I can't hear you!" shouts Tim. "Sing a song or something!"

I start in with the first thing that comes to mind. "O Come All Ye Faithful." They join me. You know, the doctor has a nice tenor voice. The nurse can't carry a tune at all, but she's loud. The smoke starts to clear.

"A sprightly number, that is. D'you do requests?" Hat, orange coat, boots, mask, it's a firefighter of course. "This way, quick now!" He's unwrapping me. "We've set up an emergency chute here, it'll be faster than the ladder. And safer."

"What happened?" asks the doctor. "How did it start?"

"God knows." The firefighter carries me over to the window. "Get outside with you now, and well done bringing this poor lad out." Meaning me. "Any of the other patients alive?"

"Who — knows?" The doctor doesn't say who cares, but that's what he's thinking. The firefighter stares at him a minute before settling me on the chute. A bang, a jolt, and suddenly I'm cold. Cold air on my face, cold hands picking me up. Don't think I'm complaining. Thanks, I tell the firefighter at the base of the chute. He passes me to a medic.

I hear thunder, look up. The sky is almost black. The wind is dank and chill. It's rained hard and will again any minute. It's a beautiful day.

Fire trucks are everywhere. Lights flashing, radios crackling, firefighters running around. I hear them talking. "Lightning bolt shorted the main circuit," I hear. "Backup system overloaded." Then, "Most of the main floor in flames."

I see some familiar faces, most of them on stretchers, coughing. They look lost without their cough syrup. I can't find Joe. I wonder, did they get his body out. I can't find Spawn of Satan either. The medic takes me over to where there are blankets and hot drinks and makes me sit down. I'm fine, I tell him. He wraps a blanket around my shoulders, tells me to report to the big ambulance down the street.

I hear Dr Royal arguing. "These are *my* patients," he says. "I take full responsibility for them. They're part of an important research project that depends on their isolation and I won't have any of them moved without being consulted. Especially the man I came out with, Mitchell is his name. His condition is absolutely critical, and I want to know where he is at all times. If he's in the ambulance now, keep him there until I've seen him."

I stand up and start to slide away. All I have in the world is a pair of smoke-stained pyjamas and a blanket, and the blanket is borrowed, but I don't want to hang around. I look back at the building. Smoke is pouring out of the windows and the roof is steaming. Firefighters on ladders are pissing on the place next door. There's a crowd of people standing as close as they dare. Police tell them to move back and they do, for a bit.

"Here you are, lad, you'll be needing this." It's my friend the firefighter. He's carrying a coat, I wonder whose. It fits pretty well. Thank you, I say.

"All part of the TFD service. Here, button up the collar, that'll keep the worst of it out." The worst of what, I wonder. "Got to be going now, I'm on duty. I'll just wish you good luck," he says, striding off.

The fire shows itself now, leans out of the main-floor window throwing its arms in the air, saying, ha ha. A child is crying. I can hear her over the fire and the crowd going ooh, and the police telling everyone to stay back please. The front door is open. The firefighters don't move.

I stand up straight. So do all the hairs on my body. I have to do it, I don't know how or why. I run towards the building. No one sees me for the longest time, which is just as well, because it takes me the longest time to get to the door. Then someone says, "Look, over there!" A megaphone bawls, "Stop, you there! Stop!" The child keeps crying. I scramble through the doorway. Long whips of flame reach around and smack against the outside of the building. Missed me.

The hallway is filled with smoke. I know where I am. The child's room is to the left. How do I know. But I do. Don't worry, I shout. I'm coming.

"Help!" It's her voice. I'd know it anywhere. The fire is right in front of me, blocking my way. "Help!" she screams. "Help me, daddy!"

I can't bear it. I stumble into the fire.

The room is as I remember it, walls painted pink and white, bed with a frilly spread, dresser with knobs. My eyes are streaming from the smoke. There's a strong smell of burning. Maybe it's me. I know where she'll be. Not in the bed. Not on the floor. Not by the window. I move farther into the room. "Help!" she screams.

I pull open the closet door. She's curled up on the floor in her best nightie, with her bathrobe and Minnie Mouse slippers on. I grab her and put her under my coat. I can hear the fire sneaking up behind me. I take a deep breath and jump through the window into our front garden.

No I don't. The window has bars on it. I bounce off them and fall onto the floor. I'm in an office, not a bedroom, and flames are rolling towards me. My feet are burning, I'm cough-ing up my lungs and under my coat I have — no time to check what I have. I stagger back through the fire and the smoky hallway to the front door. I can't go on. I fall through the open door, crawl forward and then stop. If the fire wants me, it can have me. I'm too tired.

I hear voices asking who I am, whether I'm dead or badly burnt. They're hopeful, but I don't know what they're hoping for. I hear snicks and snacks, clicks and clacks. And a single authoritative voice saying, "Get those photographers away." Something moves under my coat. I reach inside.

"Oh, look!" they say. "See what he's got!"

"He went in to rescue it!" And more clicks and clacks. I open my eyes and find myself staring at a small gray kitten with a dirty white front.

Next thing I know I'm sitting against a fire truck, breathing into a bag. A firefighter, not my friend with the accent, is kneeling beside me. The kitten is on my shoulder. Photographers and newspeople are everywhere, making plans for me, waving microphones and teeth.

People are clapping. "You're a hero!" someone says.

The firefighter leans towards my ear. "You're a fucking idiot," he says very softly. "Risking your life for a handful of fur." Not a cat lover. The funny thing is, neither am I.

"Ah Mitchell, there you are." Dr Royal stands in front of me. His face shines with soap and he's found his smile again. "It's time for us to be getting along. You must be exhausted."

No, I say. I feel like a kid fighting the inevitable bedtime.

"Don't be difficult. The arrangements are all made. I've

called Pharm Trex and they're sending a limousine. Excuse us, please," he says to the newspeople. "This man is my patient and I'm afraid he's had all he can take for today. I speak," impressively, "as his doctor."

'm worried. He looks so powerful, standing with his legs apart and his arms folded. He looks like he's never heard the word No. He has a car and a place to sleep and a wallet, and he knows everything. I don't have anything, I don't know anything. I'm afraid the newspeople will do what he says and he'll find me another clinic and another dose of whatever it was, and I'll die. But it doesn't work out like that.

"Get out of the shot," they tell him.

"You don't understand, this man, Mitchell, is in my care, he's part of an important research project. I won't have him bothered."

One of the newspeople shoves a camera into my face and asks am I bothered. No, I tell her. Dr Royal starts to get mad.

"You fool," he says, "Mitchell here is sick. He's not competent to answer questions. If you want an interview, ask me. I was there too."

The woman doesn't back down an inch. She has basketfuls of red hair, and eyes that make you feel like she's walking on you in high heels. "Are you sick?" she asks me.

I shake my head. I used to have a cough, I say, but it's gone.

"Anything wrong with you now?"

I'm poor, I tell her. She laughs. One of the camera guys is

smiling. I could use a pair of shoes, I say. And a drink.

"Me too," she says. "Why don't we go back to my office and have it." Okay, I say.

"But you don't understand," the doctor begins. She cuts him off.

"No, doctor, *you* don't understand. He doesn't have to go with you, doesn't have to take his medicine, doesn't have to do anything he doesn't want to. He's got rights. Besides, he's the hero of the day and you're just another jerk." She turns to me. "Do you want to stay with this guy?" I shake my head. "Right, then. You're coming to the studio with me. Miles! Let's go. Nicky, see if you can get an official statement from the deputy fire chief. Mitchell, come on. My name's Theresa, by the way." We shake hands. Hers is like armour plate.

The doctor tries one more time. "Mitchell," he says, "I saved your life back there."

I stare at him. I'll owe you, I say.

They drive me a dozen blocks across town to be interviewed. Do I get a limousine. I do not. I get a jeep with letters on the side and a driver dressed worse than me. That's Miles, I guess. He drives like he smokes, and he smokes about a hundred miles an hour. We pass by hotels and big theatres. All the streets have boy names from the Bible, John Peter Timothy Duncan, names like that. Everyone is young and black from behind. When they turn around some of them look older and paler.

Theresa leads me through big glass doors into a cold, stone lobby. People shake my hand, press against me. I don't like it. Someone gets me a sweatshirt. I have to take off the fireman's raincoat to put it on. I start to shiver. Some kind of reaction. The sweatshirt has letters on it, like the jeep. Theresa pushes me through the lobby, through a busy office, and into a room with bright lights where some more people are waiting for us. At least I feel warmer. We start to play twenty questions, only they ask all the wrong questions. Do they ask about the place that caught fire or why everyone seems to have a bad cough. No. They ask about the damn cat.

"What's her name?" they ask in their deep voices. They all have deep voices, even the women. Don't know, I say.

"How long have you had her?" Who, I say.

"The kitten." But it's not mine, I say. They keep handing me the thing, and I keep putting it down.

"Were you frightened?" Yes.

"How did you feel when you found her?" Who.

"The kitten, of course." I felt funny, I say.

We take a break here for lunch. I guess it's lunch, it's sandwiches. I have no idea what time it is. Theresa disappears. I'm sitting in a folding chair with wires all around. There's a water glass in front of me. Water. I checked.

"Why did you go into the burning building?" Big pause here, suspense, our viewers want to know. "Why did you do it?" The kitten jumps into my lap. Clicks and clacks from the cameras, mmms and aaahs from the misters.

I made a mistake, I say. I drop the kitten onto the floor.

"Are you sorry to leave the Pharm Trex Faith and Charity Research Foundation and Mission?" they ask. I guess I look blank. "The place you were staying — didn't you know the name?"

I'd forgotten the name. No, I'm not sorry to leave.

"Where will you live now?" Don't know.

I'm a disappointment to them, I can tell. They're frowning, all except Theresa, who comes back and sits right beside me with a wide smile on her face.

"Would you like a drink?" she asks. A good question finally, but the rest of them look embarrassed.

"Come on, Theresa," someone says to her. "Leave the poor guy alone."

"What d'you mean?" she protests. "Here's a man who'll take a drink. We drag him away from his home, question him for hours and offer him nothing in return except a sweatshirt and some sandwiches."

"But," says one of the misters, "he'll be on the news."

"He doesn't care about the news," she says, standing up suddenly. "Look at him. Is this a man who watches the news? He's got better things to do with his time. Would you like a drink, Mitch. I've got a bottle in my office and it must be getting on to the cocktail hour. Heroism and then all this talking — it's enough to give a man a thirst." Sure, I say.

We leave together. "Wait! Hey!" They call me back. "You forgot your kitten." It's sitting on the floor, washing itself.

It's not my kitten, I say. It just follows me about.

Theresa's office is made of windows. I see a lot of rooftops and dirty sky. "What do you drink?" she says.

I figure she's not talking about cough syrup. Anything, I say. Anything at all. She pours rye into two thick glasses and gives me one. "Drink as fast and as much as you like," she says. "But I want you to be able to talk."

Well, I can talk as long as she can pour.

"Happy days," she says, raising the glass. I take a good-sized gulp and smile across the desk. I've forgotten about this stuff. I take another gulp.

She smiles too. I can see lights flashing on the CN Tower through the window. "So you're a vagrant who saves a cat. Today's news. Big deal. Tomorrow the Queen Mother is christening a new oil tanker, there's a nasty storm blowing in from the Midwest and the Red Sox are in town. Film at ten. No one's going to care about you and your kitty. Right?" Right, I say.

"You happy with that?" she says. "Drifting by to save a cat, drifting away again, no place to go, no one to care about you, the most important thing in your day the price of a drink — you like that life?" She refills my glass. I don't say anything.

"Look like a bum, smell like a bum, think like a bum — you've sure got the part down. But then you've had, what, twelve years of practice, haven't you."

Her eyes are bright bright blue. I've seen flowers that blue — but the flowers were softer. "I'm right, aren't I, Doctor Mitchell," she says. "It's been twelve years since you were in the news because of a fire."

My drink's gone again, how did that happen. I swallow anyway.

"It was about this time of year too. You left your job soon afterwards. Burnt kids are a city reporter's dream. Too bad I was covering high-school sports."

Does everyone know, I ask.

She shakes her head. "I'd forgotten. I ran your name through our subject files out of habit. No one else'll bother. You're just a human interest story. They're already worried about the Queen Mother." And the weather, I think. And the Red Sox.

"I'm not interested in raking up the past. But I have a feeling about you. There's a story somewhere, I know it." She stabs me with her gaze. "I want you to satisfy my curiosity. I'm a reporter; I want to know what makes people tick. So tell me about yourself. Why did you become a doctor? Why did you go into that building? I want to know what you were thinking about, what you were feeling. Put it into words. Remember for me. I want to know."

I'm starting to feel the liquor already, out of practice I guess. It's good, I can tell from the label, but you know, it doesn't taste very different from the cough syrup. Your idea won't work, I tell her.

She nods. "Keep talking," she says. "Start at the beginning. Why did you become a doctor?"

I don't know what she means, I never decided to become a doctor. I never decide anything, it just happens to me. And I don't know what she's expecting from one bottle of whisky, I've had thousands and I still don't remember. But I don't mind trying. She leans forward to fill my glass again.

Some days you can do no wrong. Flesh slices cleanly, blood pours away from and not into the incision, you peel back, reach in and find — *it*, whatever it is, right away, as if you could see through people. Time moves slowly. You anticipate everything from umbilical strangulation to the nurse's hiccups, you stitch like a Singer patent, and every now and then you look up to see that your colleagues are honestly enjoying themselves. The OR hums like a well-lubricated machine: in out scrub, in out scrub. I call them jewel days. You hold creation in your fingers, beautiful and precious, and finite as so many carats of carbon. I'm sure artists have these days too, and mystics and athletes and vice-presidents and waiters. As a doctor I wish I had more of them. On days like that no one dies.

They wheeled Magda into the OR in the middle of a jewel day. Two Caesareans, a hysterectomy, and a cyst that was supposed to be easy but wasn't and I knew it wouldn't be, didn't look right, didn't feel right, and if I hadn't prepped extra units of plasma she'd have gone into operative shock from the forty-point drop in base bp — *Not your fault, doctor, no one could have predicted it, just one of those things*, God I hate hearing that, while her husband is out there in the waiting room reading the sports page and thinking she'll be home soon. Yesterday or to-morrow she would have died, but today was special.

So I was feeling pretty good when Magda was wheeled in. Certainly better than she was. She was in labour. I'd decided to try induction before going in myself. At twenty-five weeks it wouldn't take long. With any luck we'd get everything at once. Cutting was a last resort. Do you mind the idea of a scar, I'd asked her. Her face had tightened. She minded. I don't want anything to remind me of the little bastard, she'd said.

"Magda O'Neill," the floor nurse read out from the chart. "Induced labour, probable stillbirth." O'Neill was the name she'd registered under. I said hello but she wasn't paying any attention to me. The nurse drew me aside.

"O'Neill didn't want an anaesthetic," she whispered importantly, her eyes glinting. "I told her you'd okayed it, but she said no. Said she wanted to know what she was doing." I went back to the table. Sweat was pouring off Magda. Her hands were balled into fists as she grunted and strained. The two OR nurses beside her whispered encouragement. She ignored them.

"How long now?" the resident asked me. Five or ten minutes, I said. She checked her notes hurriedly.

"Are you sure? Labour's barely begun. She was induced less than twelve hours ago. She could be in transition for awhile yet." Together we watched a long contraction with lots of movement. Magda barely groaned. One of the nurses wiped her face.

She's ready, I said.

"Shall I examine her?"

I shook my head. We'll be able to go on to the next section in half an hour, I said. Why don't you take your break now. You've been working hard. And take one of the nurses with you. I can finish with one pair of hands.

She stared over the top of her mask. "You mean it?" I smiled and waved her out the door.

The phone rang. Anaesthesiology was still waiting. I told him no thanks.

"What if you have to cut?" I won't, I said.

"But what if you do?" Then I'll call you, I said. He hung up, grumbling.

"That's it, Magda," the remaining nurse was saying. "you're doing good." Her name was Adele. She'd come from Newfound-land to study and you could still hear it in her voice. She was in her late twenties, a few years older than her peers, chunky, competent and the possessor of a generous chuckle.

"Am I?" Magda's first words. Her eyes were closed. She gasped as the contraction broke over her like a wave. Adele wiped her face.

When it happened it was very fast. Three pushes and he was out, head, neck and shoulders, all the rest. No ripping at all. He was small, maybe three and a half pounds, and barely alive. His lungs struggled inadequately. I cut the cord and put him aside. Not long now, I thought.

"Is it alive?" Magda tried to sit up.

Adele eased her down and asked her to push again. "There's

all the baggage to come after the passenger," was the way she put it. Magda strained. "That's good," said Adele, frowning slightly, "but we're not quite done yet." This was the tricky part.

I was confident. One more good push, I told Magda, just one, and everything will come out at once. Push down hard and steady and don't stop pushing until I tell you.

"Is it alive?" she asked again.

Yes, I said. Push now. And she pushed, and it all came out just like I said it would.

Adele looked up from the bloody bed. "That's everything, isn't it?" she asked me. I nodded.

"Now I want to see it," Magda said, raising herself with an effort. I opened my mouth to speak but she cut me off. "Let me see it."

Adele frowned. I reached for the body to show Magda.

"It's a boy," she said. "I thought it might be." She stared for a moment. "He's dead, isn't he."

But he wasn't. He moved. His lungs were puny under-developed little bags that didn't work properly yet, but he was filling and emptying them as fast as he could. He cried in my arms, the pathetic mew of a small sick baby. It gets me no matter how often I hear it. I could feel him starting to go. Without even knowing what I did I wrapped him in a blanket. My hands were shaking.

"Oh ... oh." Magda slumped sideways. Quickly we laid her back on the pillows and checked her vital signs. Pulse and respiration normal, pressure normal, no bleeding, colour beginning to return. She'd fainted. We covered her and then looked at each other. And at the baby. He was a trier. It occurred to me that we must have got Magda's dates wrong. He might be as much as twenty-seven weeks.

Dammit, I said. I don't know who I was talking to. I can't do it.

Adele nodded wordlessly.

Not like this, I said. Not today.

That's how decisions are made. Yesterday, tomorrow, I might have let him go. Yesterday, tomorrow, he might already be dead. Adele phoned down to the Intensive Care Unit. He was going to need help. There was some apparatus along the far wall for the C-sections we'd done earlier. I suctioned him, gave him oxygen. I hoped I wasn't too late. No, that's not true — I knew I wasn't too late.

Adele hung up. "They're ready," she said. "Someone will be along in a minute."

We put Magda on a gurney without speaking. Adele arranged the blankets and wheeled her, still unconscious, to the recovery room. I stared down at her son, counting the quick laboured breaths, until the ICU nurse came for him.

The only chair in the scrub room was a rickety old thing on castors. I sat down carefully. My legs wouldn't hold me up any longer. Adele came up behind me and gave my shoulder a squeeze.

"He'll make it, won't he." I nodded.

"Thought so. You have any children, doc?"

One on the way, I said. Almost this far along.

"Oh. Is that why ..." her voice trailed away.

I shook my head again. Never thought about it, I said.

"Well, anyway — thanks, doc."

I looked up. Her face creased into a smile.

"I thought someone should thank you. I mean, she's not going to thank you, poor screwed up kid. Neither will her parents. And Dr Treadway sure won't." I had to smile myself. Jeff Treadway was the pediatrician in the ICU, a stickler for order, paperwork, permissions. I had no idea what I was going to tell him, but I knew that it wouldn't be good enough.

"So I thought I'd say thanks. Maybe some day he'll be able to thank you himself."

Maybe, I said. I stripped off my gloves and plunged my hands into hot water.

Treadway wasn't happy at all. "It's irresponsible," he told me. Dr Treadway didn't swear. Irresponsible was the worst thing he could say about you and he'd said it three or four times already. "The child is fourteen weeks premature. Barely viable. I've had to use all the technology there is and the situation is still touch and go. Maybe he isn't brain damaged. Maybe. And now, hours later, I find out that the decision to act aggressively was yours alone. The boy was supposed to be a stillbirth. I'm disappointed, doctor." Disappointed was another one of his words.

How do you think he feels, I said.

"This isn't a laughing matter." Of course, for Treadway nothing was a laughing matter. "You should have taken the wishes of his mother — your patient — into account."

His office was just down the hall from Intensive Care. Filing cabinets covered all four walls, making the room seem even smaller than it was. Treadway had thin lips and a small, neat nose. He sat perfectly straight, tapping his In-Tray with a pencil, wishing he could get on with emptying it. I drew deeply on my cigarette. I thought I understood what was bothering him. It's the irregularity, isn't it, I said. All those blank spaces on the forms.

"Don't make fun, young man," he snapped. No more than

ten years my senior, he seemed from another generation with his unfashionably short hair and dark suits. "Your actions today have made things difficult for me."

I'd had enough. Come on, Treadway, I said. How hard can it be. Look after him for two or three months and he'll be a healthy male infant. He'll be adopted in no time.

"And meanwhile all that care and attention is being paid for by the long-suffering overburdened province." Treadway might have been talking about his mom. "You're a cowboy, Mitchell. You think you can doctor better than the rest of us. It would do you good to have to run the hospital yourself."

The funny thing was that Treadway was himself a really great doctor, caring, sensitive, ruthlessly aggressive when the situation demanded it. But behind a desk he turned into Administration Man. I put my hand on his In-Tray. Caught his attention. Leaned over the desk and spoke from down deep. Thanks, Treadway, I said. That shut him up.

Old man Opara was expecting my call. I got through right away. After assuring him about his daughter, I mentioned that the baby lived.

"Really," was all he said. I sensed a lot of emotion in the ensuing silence.

I'm afraid things are a bit complicated, I said. He'll have to stay in hospital a few months before being put up for adoption.

More silence. Then, "Is the boy in danger?" I was surprised at his interest.

Every hour he lives improves his chances, I said. He's in a special nursery now. He'll move to a regular nursery when his breathing improves.

"And my daughter is well, you say? Recovering nicely?"

Yes, sir, I said. I'm on my way to look in on her now.

"Good. Good. Er, doctor." Something he wanted to ask. "This baby. This boy. Tell me more about him."

What, I wondered. He's small, hairless, nearly dead, with fifteen wires taped to skin so fragile he bleeds when the tapes are pulled away. He's a strong boy, I said. A real fighter. He just wouldn't quit.

"He gets that from me," murmured Opara. Pride in his voice, and wonder. And tears, I'd bet. "My grandson."

Tears for sure now.

I was late for dinner again but Lucy didn't mind. We sat at the kitchen table together. I had warmed-up meat loaf and scotch on the rocks, she had a glass of milk as I told her the whole story. Now that Opara wanted to keep the baby himself I could use real names.

Her eyes shone. Beautiful eyes she had, small and so intensely blue that they sometimes looked almost black. "That's wonderful," she said. "The poor lonely man will have someone to love. And the little baby will have a grampa who loves him. It's like something out of Dickens."

Dickens made it simple, I said. He killed all the moms in childbirth. Magda really hates the boy. It's not an ideal situation.

"Better than an institution. Better than being dead." Lucy brought the argument back to earth. But I remembered a pretty teenager with rain-damped hair sitting in my office, a disturbed young woman who'd wanted to watch her baby die. Did Leon Opara have any idea of his daughter's state of mind, I wondered.

"You saved a life today, darling," said Lucy. "Are you sorry?" Poor baby, clinging to existence by a slim, medically assisted thread. Still fourteen weeks until he'd be old enough to be born.

Sometimes it all makes sense, I said. And sometimes it's just a mess.

"I'm sure God feels the same way."

The change from Baby O'Neill, unwanted, fighting for his life, to Leon Opara Junior, darling of the Special Nursery, was swift and complete. Amazing what an influential grandfather will do for your popularity. I used to check on the baby myself, from time to time — call it a parental feeling. In a real sense he was my baby as much as Magda's or Opara's, almost as much my baby as my own Cheryl Ann, who was born without fuss or complication on a snowy morning in February, shortly after little Leon graduated to the regular nursery. I was present as a father, held Lucy's hand, told her to do what she was already doing, bothered the nurses, cried when the obstetrician held out the little dark-headed bundle.

"He's sweet, isn't he," Lucy said to the doctor.

"But, Mrs Mitchell, your baby is a girl."

"I meant him." Pointing at me.

My career star continued to rise. More time in the OR, more space on the floor, more power in committees. My own office right next to Cochrane's. Opara never thanked me for going against his and his daughter's expressed wishes and giving him a grandson. We never spoke about it. But he made a point of praising me, talking me up to visiting dignitaries, re-commending me for this and that, making sure I got invited to functions. As a result my practice grew in size and – I don't know how else to put it – social status. I had a waiting list and two receptionists.

Lucy laughed and laughed when I told her I was redecorating. I had to smile too, her amusement was so genuine. And I knew that she was just as genuinely pleased for me. "My husband, the society doctor."

Anything but that, I said with a little shiver and a glance at the wall where we'd hung mother's picture.

The society doctor. That was what my mother had called me the previous month, the only time she ever visited the house. With a shake of her head as if to say, What a waste. I wanted to shout, Isn't that what you wanted me to be. Aren't you proud. She'd brought a gift, a Huron depiction of the Holy Family's flight into Egypt. A winter scene, snow and bare trees, Mary and Joseph in furs, the papoose on Mary's back.

My office really does need new furniture, I said.

"Of course it does, darling." She settled the baby in the

crook of her arm, soothing it against her breast. The evening feed was my favourite, I made a point of getting home for it. No frantic sucking, none of the bullying that babies are so good at. The two of them seemed content with each other. It was playful, a relaxed conversation between equals. I got up to empty the ashtray.

I can't let Mrs Fosdyke sit in a moulded plastic chair, I said.

"Of course not, dear. She might not know how."

And Mrs Wellman's sable coat doesn't look right on a wooden peg, I said.

"How does it look on Mrs Wellman?"

I had to smile. The answer was: authentic. Waddling along in her coat Mrs Wellman really did resemble a large fur-bearing animal. Her family owned a chain of department stores and she had friends in the opera gala charity auction Tory fundraiser circuit — many of whom had become my patients.

"Never mind, darling. I'm proud of you. Mrs MacGillivray herself called me up to say how very much she liked you, and she's the snootiest of my mother's friends. 'Such gentle hands,' she said, 'but I expect you already know about them, don't you, Lucy.'"

Frankly, I enjoyed my bit of local celebrity. The first time we got our picture in *Toronto Life* magazine I bought a dozen copies. It didn't mean as much to Lucy, who had been smiling for fashion photographers since she was six years old. But I did come across a copy of the magazine, months later, in her desk drawer.

I lost touch with Magda. At her post-partum visit she was withdrawn and quiet. She was dressed casually, her hair was short, dirty and uncombed. Unlike her son, she'd lost weight and without makeup she looked almost haggard. I asked about school.

"Oh, I'm not going this year. Psychiatric leave," she said, rolling her eyes.

How about modelling, I said.

"Look at me." She gestured helplessly. "Who'd want me as a model — except maybe undertakers. What the well-dressed corpse is wearing." She didn't laugh. Physically, she was in pretty good shape. I told her so. All she needed was a few good meals, I said, and a few nights' sleep. I asked if her psychiatrist was prescribing anything for her.

"Lots," she said, but didn't elaborate. I brought the baby into the conversation deliberately, wanting to know how she felt about him.

"Oh, little Leon," she said. "Yeah, I hear he's doing real well. He'll be coming home soon. Dad's having the north wing of the house made over for him."

She hadn't been to see him in the hospital. I asked if she wanted to.

"No no. Dad can visit for both of us. He's dad's baby, you know — the son he never had." She smiled too calmly. I wanted to reach out to her somehow, assure her that someone cared what became of her, but at that moment my nurse poked her head into the examination room. Mrs Sheldrake had checked herself into the hospital. Labour was active, contractions four minutes apart. I'm on my way, I said.

Magda was already putting on her coat. I asked if she wanted to see me again soon, just to chat. "You sound like my psychiatrist," she said. "And anyway, I'm going on a cruise next week. With a girlfriend. I wanted to go alone but dad wouldn't let me. I don't know if he's afraid of suicide or another pregnancy." She laughed. I tried to smile.

"**Y**ou're not helping me," says what is her name, the newswoman. I've forgotten her name. "You're not remembering the right things," she says. "I want to know about you and the fire, and all you can tell me about is someone named O'Neill and an old operating-room melodrama."

Not O'Neill, I say. Opara. Leon Opara. What a piece of trash he turned out to be. And he should have gone to jail, but that was later, I say.

"Really?" She perks up like a hound dog on a fresh scent. "I didn't hear you say that before. Leon Opara. His name was in your news file." She's standing over me, whatever her name is. Now she goes back to the desk. "Wait a minute. It says here that Opara helped your career. He recommended you for all sorts of things — there's even a picture of the two of you shaking hands, I didn't see that before." She looks over at me, shakes her head. "Not that anyone would recognize you."

Theresa, that's her name. I remember now.

"So why should Leon Opara go to jail?" she asks. I don't answer right away. The whisky bottle's half full. Not me, I'm half empty.

Her lips are wet. She types something into her computer,

waits. "Here he is. Address on Post Road. Of course. Clubs, societies, blah blah. Director of this and that. Donates a million to the United Way. Builds a theatre. Gives a new wing to the Civic Hospital." She looks over at me. "That was your hospital before they kicked you out. You and Opara were both on the board. Is there a connection? What do you know about Opara's problems? Was it taxes or fraud or something else?"

What do you mean, I say. He's ten years old. How many ten-year-olds have tax problems. Theresa slumps back in her chair. Violence, I say. Assault with a firearm. He shot another kid in the leg. I should know.

"Leon Opara is one of the most respected men in the city. You're saying he shot a child? How do you know?"

I wave my hand. Not that Leon Opara, I say. The other one. His grandson. I'm hungry, I say. And I'm getting a headache.

"Me too."

The door opens and someone walks in. "Hey there, Theresa," he says. His voice is all buttery. "Don't you know what time it is?"

"Hi, Bryn," she says.

"You've been drinking," says Bryn. "And your office stinks of smoke! I could smell it outside. And — who's that?"

"He's the hero of the hour. The man who saved the kitty from the Faith and Charity Mission fire this morning. He's why the office is smoky," she adds.

"Oh yes." Bryn stares at me from under long brown lashes. "The Pharm Trex mission. They use it for human experiment-ation, don't they," he says. "Drug therapy. Diphtheria — no, TB. We did a feature on them last year." I sit up straight. I try to sit up straight.

"You really shouldn't get too close to him," he says.

I can't speak. Everyone knew what was going on. I try to imagine the feature, tasteful interviews with Dr Royal, shots of him holding a needle full of whatever it was. You wonder about democracy sometimes. What kind of government lets this stuff happen to its people. I'm glad I don't vote. I'd be afraid I'd pick the winner.

"Terry, " he says, "why don't you ditch this human ashtray and come home." Manners. Bryn must do their good manners segments.

"Actually, honey, I have to stay here a bit longer."

"What?" He pouts. Years since I saw anyone do that. "Well, if you prefer him to me." He pauses. Theresa doesn't say anything. Bryn goes out, slams the door.

"You just dropped out of sight," Theresa says to me. "One week a front-page headline, the next week a question mark. Not that I blame you. I can understand wanting to run away. God, your family and your career just vanishing like that — it'd be enough to turn anyone's mind inside out." She leaves a pause here for me to fill. I'm thinking about my headache and the bottle on her desk. I don't say anything.

"I want to know how it happened, what you thought then and what you're thinking now, all these years later. I want to know why you walked into the fire today. And I know you can tell me. You're not a typical derelict," she says. Compliments now. "You're a highly educated man. Somewhere behind those glazed eyes is a real mind. Now, doctor, what do you say?

Would you like another drink?" She points at the bottle.

"I know alcohol helps," she says. "The people who say you drink to forget don't understand. You drink to remember, don't you: who you really are, what really happened to you. You forget about today, sure you do, but if you're a real drinker today is usually worth forgetting."

The bottle looks nice. I'm thirsty — not real thirsty, but enough. She pours herself a drink. Her eyes glitter. I'm hungry too, I say.

She nods. "I know. But if I get you some food you'll just fall asleep. I want you awake and remembering." No, I say.

She takes a gulp, licks her lips. "Good stuff."

You have any trouble looking at yourself in the mirror, I say. She smiles. Remembering won't do me any good, I say.

"I don't want you to remember for your sake," she says. "Do it for me."

I don't understand, I say.

"What do you care? D'you want a drink or not?" She uncaps the bottle, tilts it. The brown tide swims up towards the rim, hovers over my empty glass. I reach out.

"Think back," she whispers. "Tell me things."

She pours. I drink. I'm not hungry any more. "Remember," she whispers.

I can't, I say. She pours again. I drink again.

"Remember."

There's brown in my glass, and then there isn't, and then there isn't any glass.

We were all invited to a lunch party at the Oparas in honour of little Leon's sixth birthday. The Opara house was a bit of merrie England in the heart of Upper Canada. Not such a little bit, either, a few acres of deer park and a Northamptonshire manor had been transplanted tree by tree and stone by stone — and for all I knew deer by deer. Even Lucy was impressed. Cheryl Ann was excited because she had a real party dress to wear. There were tights and shoes to go with it. Lucy had a new dress too. I wore a tuxedo. The invitation said to.

Grandfather and grandson met us at the huge front door. The boy's tux looked better than mine. I admired it. "Took him to my Savile Row bespoke tailor," his grandpa told us over a tall fluted glass of champagne and orange juice. Not my favourite drink, but I smiled and took it anyway. Next thing I knew Cheryl Ann was on the floor, howling.

"What happened, honey?" Lucy picked her up. She was never too far away.

"He pushed me."

"Not very hard," said Leon. "She practically fell over all by herself." Grandpa guffawed. Lucy blinked and took Cheryl Ann's hand.

"We'll make sure you don't fall again," she said smoothly.

"But I didn't fall, mommy. He pushed me. He did."

"How would you like some orange juice," said Lucy, leading her away.

Opara ruffled his grandson's hair. "Boy's got spunk," he said.

More guests were arriving. A servant came up with a tray. "I want some champagne too, Baxter," Leon demanded. The servant hesitated. "Give me some. Come on!" The boy lashed out with his foot. Baxter looked at Opara for help.

"Better give him some." An indulgent smile. "He'll just keep kicking you until you do."

The spacious elegance of the ballroom had been turned into a pinball arcade for the day. Opara had rented dozens of machines and the place echoed with noises of electronic victory and defeat. The effect was unsettling and faintly comic, like biting into a martini olive stuffed with a licorice allsort. A few kids were running around and jumping on each other, but most were absorbed in solitary struggles against wizards and aliens. It was the complete boy's fantasy guide to life. I remember thinking how lonely little Leon must be. He spent most of the party pushing smaller kids off games he wanted to play. Lucy wasn't the only mom to stick close to her youngster.

At the end of the party Opara shook hands with Lucy and me and Leon shook hands with Cheryl Ann. She giggled when he stuck out his tongue at her. In the car I asked if she'd had a good time. "Oh yes," she said. "He's a funny boy, isn't he?"

Hilarious, I agreed.

We talked about it later. "That boy is something else," Lucy said. "You know, I saw him push Cheryl Ann down. One of the servants actually ran out of the room when Leon came up to him."

Poor Baxter. Of course it's his grandfather's fault, I said, spoiling him like that.

"I wonder if that's true. In the case of a bad child, it's interesting the way we automatically look to the parents. Spoiling, not paying enough attention, mental or physical abuse — no end to the harm parents can do. But if the same child is well-behaved, we say: What a nice boy. What a nice girl. We don't say: He must have marvellous parents. I sometimes wonder if good and bad aren't part of the package along with black hair and brown eyes and a beautiful tenor voice."

That's a little simple, don't you think, I said.

"I'm a simple woman. And I know that environment counts for a great deal, but you can't teach the blind to drive. You can't win a basketball game with a viola section. Not often, anyway."

So little Leon is bad because he's a bad kid. One of nature's mistakes. Is that it, I said. I found a cigarette.

"Darling, are you upset?"

No, I said shortly.

"Is it the boy? Leon?"

No.

"He isn't your responsibility. He may be here thanks to you, but you didn't make him who he is."

I didn't say anything. Maybe that was part of it. Maybe I wanted to believe I'd done the right thing six years ago. That it wasn't my fault.

"Darling, you're a doctor. You get to play God sometimes, but it's just like a little kid dressing up in her mom's clothes: You're cute but you don't fool anyone." I smoked in silence for a bit. She was right, I guessed. Still, I wished Leon wasn't such a little shit.

"**A**nd the Hero was all by himself?" She sat up in bed, her hand reaching for mine. All by himself, I said, in a cabin in the middle of the woods. He was painting a picture of the death tree across the lake, where a murderer had been hanged long ago. It was a great big old pine tree, nearly rotten, and it had stood by itself on the rocky point for hundreds of years. As night fell, a gigantic storm came up, I said.

"Was the Hero scared?" She always asked that. She loved it that the Hero wasn't scared of anything. Of course not, I said. He kept painting while the lightning flashed and the thunder boomed out in the inky darkness and then, suddenly, he started choking. There was no one in the cabin but he felt like someone was throttling him. He thrashed around but he couldn't get free. He looked over at his picture, I said, and it was different. Now there was a hangman's rope on the lowest branch of the tree. He hadn't painted it, but it was there. And dangling from the rope was a man in a red-checked jacket just like his. And the figure was struggling and kicking and choking just like him. And the face inside the noose was — his face, I whispered.

"Hoo boy." She shivered. The Hero was in trouble, I said.

The world was going black. And then he heard, in the distance, the sound of hooves: clip clop, clip clop. It was —

By now she was bouncing up and down on the bed, clapping. "It was Princess Cheryl Ann, coming on horseback to save him!" she cried.

The formula went back a long way. Ever since she could talk I'd been telling her stories about the Hero, a big strong man who was never afraid, and who could lift anything — Even a chair? Yes, even a chair. Even that chair? Yes, even that chair — but was always getting in trouble, only to be rescued in the nick of time by the beautiful Princess Cheryl Ann.

"And I was wearing my nightie with polka dots." The princess always described what she was wearing. "And I wasn't scared either, and I went right into the cabin and I said, 'That's enough!' And I broke the picture of the hanging man."

And with a flash of lightning and a crack of thunder, the Hero was free, I said. And he and the princess went outside and saw that the old pine tree, survivor of a thousand storms, had fallen at last. And the Hero thanked the princess, who was feeling tired because it was past her bedtime.

"Oh, Daddy!"

The telephone rang when I got downstairs. Lucy was in the garage, welding. I picked up, for once not expecting an urgent summons. None of my patients was close to her due date.

Opara was terse. "I need a favour. Come over here right now."

If it's an emergency, I said, a hospital would be faster.

"No. No hospitals. I want you." I hesitated, wanting to say no, but unable to do so. Nothing Hippocratic. I felt obliged to him.

"Please." His voice was still under control. I wondered how often he'd had to ask for anything. Okay, I said.

"And doctor — bring your bag." He hung up.

Lucy shut off the blowtorch when I went out to the garage. Under the safety visor and the dirt she looked anxious. "Everything all right?" she asked.

I doubt it, I said.

No, I said. Opara frowned. His grandson looked away. I hadn't seen the boy for about four or five years. I'd heard a few things, none of them complimentary. Sounded as if they were true. No, I said again.

"He hit me first," said Leon. As if that justified everything. The three of us were in an upstairs bathroom. I was washing the blood off my hands. The boy Leon had shot was down the hall, asleep.

I never did find out his name. He was a friend from boarding school, visiting for the long weekend. The two boys got into an argument about something important to ten-year-olds — cars, I think, or some game involving cars. Tempers rose and the other boy threw a punch at Leon, who walked calmly over to his desk, pulled out a handgun and shot him in the leg. A felony. And they wanted me to cover it up.

"Just go home and forget about it, doc," said Leon. "He'll get better."

He probably would. The bullet had passed cleanly through the boy's upper calf. Blood loss was minimal. He'd hurt for awhile but there wouldn't be any permanent damage.

No, I said. I have to report it. It's the law.

"How much will you take?" said Leon with a knowing smile. "I could probably buy you a new car — would you like that?"

"Go to bed, Leon," said his grandfather with more authority than I'd seen him show towards the boy. "Go to bed right now."

"Sure, gramps. Sure. G'night, doc." He sketched a wave and sauntered down the hall. Opara sighed.

He led me down a back staircase to what I guess was a scullery. Flagstones, cupboards, copper pots, fireplace, dishwasher. I thought he was taking me out the servants' entrance. I was wrong. On the other side of the scullery was a dim passageway giving onto a surprisingly luxurious room. Leather chairs on a thick Oriental carpet, another fireplace, books, a humidor, oil paintings I'd seen reproduced elsewhere. It might have been a stage set except for the row of locked steel filing cabinets. I'd never been there before. It was, he explained, a very private office.

He poured two drinks from a beautiful, cut glass decanter, sat beside me and said, "Thanks for coming." I nodded, drank, felt better.

"I'd like to tell you a bit about young Leon. Sit there a moment and drink your Armagnac. It's good, isn't it — older than I am." He put down his drink.

"Now, the boy is a handful, I admit it. Impulsive, strongwilled, can't always control his temper — in short, a young hellion. I know I've probably made things worse, but he had such a tough start in life that I just can't seem to refuse him much. And he's so everlastingly like me when I was his age." The house was quiet. I wondered about the servants, and what they'd make of the blood in Leon's room.

"But I want you to know, doctor, that underneath that tough-guy act is a very," he paused, went on quietly, "a very good sort of boy. Sometimes he's too aloof, sometimes too boisterous. It makes him difficult to like. He doesn't make friends easily and that bothers him. His teachers soften it, say he isn't a good mixer, but I've seen the hurt. I was so happy when he told me that he'd asked someone to stay with us over the half-term holidays."

How did he come to have a gun, I asked.

"It's one of mine." Opara shook his head sadly. "We were looking at them the other evening. I must have forgotten to lock the drawer."

I'd had about enough. So, I said, we're talking about a moody kid — violent, solitary, and with access to firearms. Now tell me why I shouldn't report this gunshot wound to the authorities, as I am legally obliged to do.

Opara smiled at me. "Because you care about him, Mitchell. Why d'you think I got you here, instead of his family doctor? You can't get over bringing him into the world any more than I can. I watched you tonight. You stole his life for him and gave it to me. We're the only two people in the world who'd think about giving him another chance. Remember, once you go to the cops it's official. I'll pull some strings, but there's only so much I can do. The black mark will always be there."

Are you sure, I said. An accident like this, a ten-year-old boy overreacting —

"Trust me. Anything else that happens in his life, his fault or no, and they'll dig up what happened tonight."

What about the other boy, I said. And his parents. Opara relaxed. "His father runs a trucking business," he said. "Pretty successful, but the teamsters are acting up and he's a bit short of cash right now. He's already approached a bank whose board I sit on. Don't worry about repercussions from that end."

He poured us each another drink. "Here's luck," he said. "To us and to the boy." Luck, I echoed.

"I'm glad you agreed to help us out," he said, "before I told you about the opening on the Civic Hospital board. I knew you'd hate the idea of being bought off."

I didn't choke on my Armagnac. I swallowed carefully. Tell me about the opening, I said.

A few weeks after I'd joined the board I found myself walking down the corridor behind two of my colleagues. They were talking about Leon.

"The boy's a menace," I heard one of them say. "Do you know he's put four people in hospital. And that servant he shot — I heard Opara paid almost a million dollars to keep it out of the courts. One more affair like that and not even the old man will be able to save him from juvenile detention."

see stars in the big window, high up and fainter than the lights in the offices. They twinkle in the dark. I'm lying on the floor of Theresa's office. She frowns down at me, threatening. I don't care much. I'm threatening myself.

"I should have known better," she says. "You bums are all the same. Lousy liars. Don't know what's real half the time." She bends, gets her hands under my shoulders and lifts. "Why did I waste any time on you?" she says, and then, "Oh, shit! Not in my office." Too late, of course. I've carried out my threat. Does whisky stain, I wonder. There wasn't much else in my stomach, and now even that's gone.

"Smell like a bonfire and puke all over my rug. Cost me two bottles of whisky and a date." Theresa mutters to herself as she drags me down a hallway. No one is around. It's very quiet. "Try for an exclusive and what do I get. Leon Opara's grandson is a bad kid. Oh, it's exclusive all right." She rolls me into the elevator. There are mirrors everywhere. A hundred decrepit figures slump shapelessly on the floor, drooling, just like me. A hundred Theresas look down and sigh. And slip a bill into a hundred pockets. "So long, doctor. See yourself on the news."

But it's true, I say. He is a bad kid.

"Leon Opara doesn't have a grandson." The elevator door closes. I'm alone with the droolers.

The lobby looks different at night. Now it's a cold empty place, marble pillars and piped music. Might be a church except for the armed guard standing over me. Not too many armed guards in church.

"What I want to know is how he got in here in the first place." Is he talking to me. Probably not. "I could ask," he says, "but I don't think I'll get much out of him." Talking about me to someone named Roger. I don't hear Roger talking though. "Just double-check the fire exits on your side. And the loading bays. We don't want another piece of toast floating in."

Who's a piece of toast. I thought I'd been called everything.

"Roger," he says. "Out." The music's louder. I've heard it before, but I don't know what it is. Big glass doors nearby. The way I came in.

He squats next to me. "Hey," he says. "Hey, you." A young mister with muscles, a soft voice, and eyelashes like a girl. "How'd you get in?" he asks. I point at the big doors.

"Front entrance," he says. "You came through the front entrance?" Yes mister, I say. He moves his mouth like he doesn't believe me. "Came in one of the station's cars, didn't you," he says, "with a driver and a bunch of media types. Then you gave your own press conference. And they gave you a sweatshirt with the station's logo to wear with your pyjama bottoms and smelly raincoat. That right?" I'm wrong. He does believe me.

He stands way up, pushes a button someplace on his shirt. "Nothing doing," he says. "Poor bastard doesn't know anything. No point holding him," he says to Roger, then picks me up by the back of my coat, carries me over to a little door beside the big doors, unlocks it and dumps me on the pavement outside.

The sidewalk isn't any harder than the floor inside. Stone is stone. It's darker and colder though. And the music is gone. I get up and start to walk. I'm hungry and my bare feet hurt. Boy am I hungry. Theresa gave me enough for a donut. I could eat a donut. I look around but I don't see any donut shops. There are places with machines in the windows, places with clothes, places with books, places with secrets. There are restaurants from around the world that all look the same inside. All the doors are closed, all the lights are dim, all the people are gone. Still, I am surprised there are no donut shops.

A bus is stopped at the next big intersection. SKY DOME it says on the front. On the side is a picture of someone eating spaghetti. It looks good. I have to swallow.

The sidewalks are empty except for me and the garbage piled by the curb. Machine garbage from the stores with machines, paper garbage from the stores with books. I check through some restaurant garbage, but there is nothing I recognize except coffee grounds and cockroaches, and I don't eat either one. Doesn't anyone go out for a hamburger around here. I step on something that squishes between my toes. I don't look down.

After a couple more blocks I come to Bathurst Street and the river. Silvery reach of water running down towards the lake. I can't remember it. Been a while since I was this far west.

It's a stream really, no more than a few feet wide. A cab makes a U-turn, flinging out a great fan of water. I leap back. The cab drives away. If I can get around river I won't have to get wet. I turn away into the darkness. After awhile I reach the outfall from a broken fire hydrant. That's where the river starts — no wonder I couldn't remember it.

A sign catches my eye. Why they made it, I suppose. It's flashing, the only moving thing I can see except for the stream of water. The sign beckons through the dank air, drawing me on with the promise of — donuts.

The clock in the donut shop reads 1:30. Can that be right. I should be thinking about bed. It's a cool night, but with my feet tucked up and my new raincoat pulled around me, and some newspapers, I should be okay for a few hours. Not much happens this late at night. What time is it, I ask the waitress, an unmotherly soul with gum in her mouth and a cigarette behind her ear for afters. She works one eyebrow up and down like a barbell.

"Clock's on the wall," she says. I guess it really is 1:30. "What'cha want?"

A donut, I say.

"Came to the right place. What kind of donut?"

Any kind, I say. The door opens and a big guy comes in.

"You got any money?" the waitress says to me.

You know things are bad when the donut shop asks you for cash in advance. Course I do, I say. Reaching inside my coat pocket I have a sudden memory of the stuff I kept in my old pockets — money, coupon for a candy bar but it's only good if I buy another candy bar first, twist-ties, plastic knife. And the address Sally wrote down for me, the place on Sunnyside. I wish I hadn't lost that.

"Isn't there some kind of donut you like?" she says. I see donuts with white icing and donuts without white icing. All the donut shops I've been in, those are the only two kinds I ever see.

"Hi there," says the big guy. He's come up behind me.

"Wait your turn, Ralph," she says. But he's not talking to her. He puts his hand on my arm. Gently, like he's afraid of hurting me.

"Can I help you?" he asks me. He's a giant. I look up, all I can see is the bottom of his chin, where he hasn't shaved in a while. And nostrils like a dual exhaust. "You look like you need help. Can I buy you a donut?" Well, I say.

"This lady here doesn't recognize the dignity of poverty, as I do. She sees a bum with no shoes. Isn't that right, Bernadette?"

Her name is Bernadette. Someone has a sense of humor. "Uh huh," she says.

"Whereas I see a fellow sufferer, a fellow victim of life. No doubt you were hoping for generosity from Bernadette. A waste of time. But I can command her simply by giving her this." And he pulls out a twenty-dollar bill. "Right?"

"Uh huh," she says. She's impressed.

"I'd like a dozen cream-filled donuts, Bernadette. You don't mind, do you?" he says to me. I don't mind. "And then two coffees, double double for me and — how do you take your coffee?" I stare up at him. I can see his earlobe now, and the bottom of his sideburns. Red, thick hair. "You like cream and sugar in your coffee?" he asks. Sure, I say. "And regular for my guest," he says.

She pours and spoons, scoops the donuts into a box, puts everything on a tray, makes change, cracks her gum. A busy minute or two for Bernadette.

Holding the loaded tray in one hand, Ralph shepherds me to a table with the other. We sit down. "I'm sorry," he says, "I don't know your name." I tell him.

"I'm Ralph," he says. "Ralph Sizemore. I live just around the corner from here. In my father's house." He swallows a donut at a gulp.

His face is pointed at the top and bottom, like a football, and at least as big. It looks small on top of the rest of him. Sizemore indeed. He's a mountain. When he takes off his coat it's strip mining. I leave my coat on, take a bite of donut, a sip of coffee. The donuts have white icing on them. Not what I'd have ordered, the stuff gets on your clothes and stays there for weeks. But I'll eat them.

The sign outside flashes on and off. Ralph and I are still the only customers. Bernadette is smoking her cigarette.

Ralph is getting nervous. He plays with the stuff on the tray. He checks his watch. He takes quick breaths. He asks me if I know this part of the city well. Does he think we're on a date.

I'm not from around here, I say. I yawn. I know it's rude but I've had a long day.

Ralph pushes his chair back, all concerned. "Oh, dear," he says. "You must be feeling exhausted. Would you like a refill of coffee? Or another donut?" There's only one left. I shake my head. Ralph eats the donut. "No place to stay, either? Come home with me. I've got a spare bedroom. It's not far. We can walk it in a few minutes. What do you say, Mitch?" I don't say anything but I don't need to. He pulls me to my feet and practically carries me to the door.

"Night, Bernadette," he sings out. "See you next time." The bell over the door rings as we leave. Bernadette shakes her head.

Ralph walks fast. He seems excited, nervous, as if he's going into battle. He won't let go of my arm. "Come on, Mitch," he says. "Not far now." I think I fall asleep. I sure don't remember the last part of our walk. Next thing I know I'm teetering on top of a flight of stone steps. Ralph is panting — has he carried me up. The street below is narrow, badly lit. The houses are dark. Ralph fumbles with a key and lets us inside.

"Welcome," he says, smiling and panting, just a big good-natured old dog. "I'm really glad I met you. It was quite a stroke of luck, our running into each other in the donut shop. My analyst doesn't believe in luck, but I do. I'm always watching for it. When I saw you tonight, I knew." Really. Knew what, I wonder. I don't know anything except that I'm tired.

"First things first. A bath, don't you think?" Ralph frowns at me. "That way." He points down the corridor. The bathroom is so clean I have to blink. He runs steamy water, gets towels and carbolic soap. "You don't mind, do you?" he says. "I know the soap is harsh, it's just that you're so — pungent. Sorry." What does he think I am, a movie star. I tell him it's what I always use. It is too. He laughs and goes away, closing the door behind him.

The bathtub is as big as a car. I feel like the little girl in the Bible story where everything starts out too big and too hot and too hard, and then the bears come home. The water is dirty. No, that's me. The smiler with the clubfoot at St Pete's made us all take a bath once. Sarah, no, Mary. She washed our clothes too. And then we all went for a walk to the park. There was a fight and somebody spilled a bottle of Grateful Red. And then it rained. I remember Mary's smile sliding right off her face.

My eyes are full of soap and water when I hear Ralph come into the room. "Ah, that's good," he says. "You're looking much better now." I rinse my face and look up to see him putting my clothes in a bag. Going to wash them, I guess. He holds the bag at arm's length.

After the bath I put on a towel. There's nothing else. It goes around me twice, and over my shoulder, like an old Roman what is its name. I find Ralph in the living room. He's changed into what he wears for bed, he says, with a black terrycloth robe on top. We drink brandy out of glasses that remind me of the bathtub, they're so big. Not that I'm complaining.

"Tell me more about yourself," says Ralph. "Have you been in many fights, for instance?" He licks brandy off his lips. A few, I say.

"Have you ever been beaten up?" Sure, I say. I finish my drink. It takes both hands to tilt the glass.

Ralph is still licking his lips. "Do you like getting beat up?" he says. He's breathing fast. I shake my head.

"Do you scream and beg?" Beg for what, I say. "For them to

stop. For mercy."

Ralph must get beaten up by different people than me. Is there anything more to drink, I say. When he pours from the big fat bottle his hand shakes.

"Come with me," he says.

Nice spare bedroom he has, chairs and small tables, pictures, an enormous bed. It's got rubber sheets, doesn't he trust me. He pushes me down on the mattress, turns to go. No he doesn't. He turns to take off his robe and hang it up on a hook. It takes a minute for me to work out what's going on.

There's nothing under Ralph's robe except Ralph. He's enormous, like one of those big old ships in full sail, white and soft, and he has no hair. He isn't sleepy. Not at all. Guess how I know. He takes a condom from the pocket of his robe, unwraps it, carefully fits it on. Then rubber gloves. What next, a gas mask. Hey, I say.

"My analyst says that I have a need to dominate other men, the way I was dominated when I was small. My father hated me. Maybe that's why I look for men who are old enough to be my ... men like you, Mitch. You're so fucking pathetic." My head is whirling. I can't move.

I feel Ralph's hands on my towel. Over the shoulder and around the back and around again. He's unwrapping me like a present. "What's that?" he says. You'd think it was his first time. But he's pointing at a mark on my arm. "Oh, that must be a burn." He sounds relieved. "I thought it was a needle mark. I hate users." For a moment the what's its name on the front of the sailing ship was drooping. Now it sticks out again. "Doesn't it *hurt* being burnt?" he says, bending over to whisper in my ear. I don't say anything. "Maybe you don't feel it. Maybe you don't feel anything, Mitch. Tell me, can you feel *this*?" He hits me, hard. Oh oh.

"Are you scared?" he says. I try to scrunch up. Should I have seen this coming. Probably. He hits me again. "I'm going to make you afraid," he says, "the way I was afraid. I'm not afraid now. I'm big and brave. Look here." He twists my neck so I can see him. I don't know about brave, but he's big enough. Reminds me of a guy I knew back at St Pete's. I can't remember his name. We'd be in the showers and this guy would say, Look here, Pinocchio is telling lies.

Ralph picks me up, I might be a doll, and puts me in a sitting position. What can I do. He sits next to me and starts stroking my chest with his rubber-covered hands. Great if I was cold, but I'm not. Then he leans forward and bites my nipple. It hurts. It hurts so much it wakes me up. "Are you afraid?" he says, straightening to stare into my eyes. "Yes you are," he breathes. "I can see it. You're afraid of me. And you know what — you should be. You useless little coward!" He grabs me and puts me over his knee. "Useless." And starts spanking me on my poor bare fleshless bum. "Useless!"

Well, I've had worse. My mom and her favourite wooden spoon made me regret stealing a candy bar once. That was worse, and I had to go to confession afterwards.

He reaches around and grabs me underneath. "There," he

says huskily. "Got you." Wait a minute, I say. I try to pull away. He punches me with his free hand, hard. I stay still while he starts pumping me up and down, up and down, and all the while he's grunting and gloating. I don't like it at all. Better than being punched, but I'm probably going to get punched too. And I can't do anything. How much of a chance does a cow have against an electric milking machine. "You piece of shit," he says, still in that husky voice. "You piece of shit mother-fucking pansy cocksucker." Sticks and stones. "Come on, Ralph," he says, urging himself on. Is he getting tired. I know I am, and he's working harder than me.

Finally he throws me away. I curl up on the far edge of the bed and try to go to sleep, but he won't let me. He strides around the room calling me more names. Then he comes over to where I'm lying and grabs me. He pulls me up until I'm kneeling on the bed in front of him. "What do you think of this, Ralph," he says. I look up and see a giant penis. Reddish hairs sprout and curl around the base. Bulging veins crisscross the shaft and the swollen purple mushroom cap stretches the layer of rubber. I look away.

"Touch it," he says. "Don't be so fucking useless." He sounds angry. "Go on and touch it, Ralph." Who's he calling Ralph. I don't move. He takes one of my hands and puts it on him. "Push it up and down, like this." He shows me how. "Don't you play with yourself, Ralphie? Don't you know how?" When I try to move away he hits the side of my head. I put my hand back. "Yes," he says. "That's better. Up and down, you piece of scared shit. Oh yes. Now take it in your mouth." I make a mistake and start to say no, and when my mouth is open he forces himself in and holds the back of my head to keep me there.

I'm skewered, my head on a pole. He shoves himself in and out, in and out. My mouth is wide open, so I can breathe, but I can't. I'm choking. How do people do this. In and out, in and out. The rubber tastes like medicine. Is it supposed to make me better. There's an angry yellow boil just above the tangle of red pubic hair. It moves closer, then farther away, then closer again. Not a pretty sight but my alternatives are even worse. Ralph is breathing faster and faster, bucking against me, calling me his name. Which one of us is he being. The end comes when he pushes hard and out of rhythm. Suddenly my throat opens up and he goes down it. I have his whole penis in my mouth. I can feel his balls under my chin. My nose is nestled in his hair, touching the boil, which is the size and colour of a hard-boiled egg yolk. "Oh!" he says, holding me there, bucking forward. "Oh yes! Hang on, son! Daddy loves you. Daddy — "

I can't help myself. As sure as the tide rising, but a lot quicker, my guts heave up. That's twice in one evening. I'm going to have to watch what I eat. He shrieks and pulls away but he's too late, and before either one of us can do anything I've ralphed all over Ralph.

"Damn you," he says. He's shaking. He dabs at himself a few times. "Damn you to hell!" Is he angry. I don't know. He ignores the vomit on the bed, donut it looks like, and starts punching me. His face is all crumpled. He looks like a little kid. And speaking of little, I notice that Pinocchio is telling the truth now. Suddenly he grabs his robe and runs out of the room, slamming the door behind him. What am I going to do. I'm so tired. I crawl to a clean corner of the bed and pull the rubber sheet around me.

I don't sleep long or well. After a while I hear muttering in the background, someone talking about an earthquake. I roll over. The muttering continues, now he's talking about a fire. Happy conversation. I don't like it, I wish it would stop. I hear a scream, very loud. Then the voice starts on the weather. I'm about to fall back to sleep when I hear my name. What, I say. I open my eyes.

Ralph is standing in the doorway. "It's you!" he says. Not like it's a compliment. Well, maybe it isn't, at that.

Ralph is dressed, thank goodness. Clothes, hat, gloves, even a mask like you use when you're painting. Spray can of disinfectant in his hand. The voice in the background is still talking about the weather. Going to be a gray day, apparently. Chance of showers. Unseasonably cold.

"You're the guy from the fire, aren't you?" he says to me. His voice is a little muffled because of the mask. "The drug company place that burnt down yesterday. I just saw your picture on the morning news. That's why your clothes were scorched. You're the guy with the cat, aren't you?"

There's crusted blood on my lip. I can taste it, along with stale vomit and a faint hint of latex. Memories of Ralph. Where's the bathroom, I say.

"Don't move! You stay on that bed. You're infected. I'm not

richard scrimger

going to let you go through the house. Jesus, what a fucking mess." He's standing beside a picture of a white-haired vice-president on the wall. Ralph looks disgusted. So does the vice-president. Come to think of it, he looks like Ralph.

Where are my clothes, I say. I'm cold, all I have on is a headache.

"I buried your clothes last night." I stare at him. Then I pull the sheet around me.

Ralph is muttering to himself. "A mistake," he says. "The whole thing was a mistake. It always is a mistake. You were right, dad, you always were. I'm useless. I deserve it, I deserve it all. Oh, my mouth hurts. And my bottom. You were right. I'll get rid of him like the others. Just let me be clean and I'll never do it again. I'll never think about it again."

As he talks he's moving around the room, spraying it with disinfectant. He goes out of the room and returns with a big green garbage bag and a big green bottle of brandy. Well, I know what the brandy's for. Thanks, I say when he gives it to me.

Ralph's still talking. "I know I've promised before, but this time I mean it. I'll never never never do it again." He looks at me, looks at the bag in his hand. It's almost like he's measuring. "You ever found yourself in a dumpster?" he asks me.

Sure I say, why.

"Just checking." And he takes back the bottle and hits me over the head with it.

I'm floating, floating, the scent of plastic and brandy in my nose. I wish I had something to eat or wear. I wish I could breathe better. I wish I didn't smoke. Smoking gives you a headache. Inhibits vasomotor function, you start to gasp and the world spins around you. You shouldn't smoke in the house. If you have to smoke, go out to the garage.

God, I wish I didn't smoke.

"He's dead."

"Is not!"

"Is so! His face is all blue."

"Is not, I tell you! That cat was scratching at the bag, but it didn't eat him. Cats don't eat live meat. And see — he's bleeding from them scratches."

"He's dead! Otherwise why would he be here?"

"We're here, idiot! And we're alive."

"We're not in a garbage bag. Idiot yourself! I tell you he's dead. He's got a sheet and everything."

I open my eyes. Two of them, arguing, am I dead or not. One tall and skinny, one short and skinny. A gray day overhead, and seagulls. Hey, I say. I stand up slowly. The garbage bag falls from me. The dirty rubber sheet is all I have on.

"Shit," says the short one. "You're right. He's dead."

"Told you," says the tall one. "He's a ghost." They turn their backs and start poking through garbage. There's a world of it here, plastic bags piled together to make hills and valleys. I'm about halfway up a hill. Comfortable, if a bit fragrant. And there are all these noisy birds. I have to sit down again. I'm shivering. There's a bitter wind.

I'm down by the lake. That's where the wind is coming from. All this garbage must be landfill. Be a beautiful park in a few years, but right now it smells even worse than the water. A seagull glares at me. His mouth is full of something. Bun or something. Looks pretty good, but the gull is taking care of it. No point getting into a fight with a bird. They just fly away.

The two skinnies have moved on. Hey, I say as loud as I can. I follow them, tumbling down my hill like Jack and Jill, bumping my head. Plenty of brown paper around, vinegar too, probably, but I ignore it. It's hard walking on garbage, I keep falling in, have to pull myself out. My sheet won't stay on. Wait, I call. They don't stop walking, don't even break stride. Wait for me. I'm only a few feet behind them.

"You hear anything?" Tall asks Short.

"Just the ghost," says Short. "Wants us to wait for him."

I'm not a ghost, I say.

"He wants our help." Tall is a bit doubtful.

"They all say that."

"Says he's not a ghost."

"Sure. Skull for a head and a skeleton body, wears a sheet, lives in a garbage bag. What do you think he is, a lumberjack? Course he's a ghost. Say, do you see that?" Short points at something in a pile of loose trash. "That's brass," he says, pulling it out. "It's part of a trophy, I think. Jeb'll give us something for it. Anything underneath?"

I catch up to them. My face stings. I can feel blood trickling. My feet are cold. The sheet drags in the garbage. Can't you guys help me, I say. Short doesn't look up from his scrounging, but Tall stares for a bit, then slowly reaches a hand towards my face. His touch is gentle.

"You know," he says, "he feels alive." He looks at his hand. "And he really is bleeding."

Short's found a rope. He's down on his hands and knees, pulling. "Ghosts can do a lot of things, Colin," he says. The tall one's name is Colin. "Remember what Jeb was saying the other night about the ghost that played the trombone and offered to help with the monthly accounts. It's not all moaning and rattling chains, you know." The rope is stuck. Short pulls harder.

Maybe it's being so close to the water. Maybe the cold. I feel a sudden urge.

"He's taking a piss." Colin stares hard. Impolite, but I don't care. "Looks like the real thing too."

"Sure sure, a pissing ghost. Happens all the time. Give us a hand, Colin," says Short. "There's something on the end of this rope."

I finish. They pull together. "It's coming," says Short. No it isn't. They pull some more. Colin looks over his shoulder at me. Let me help, I say. Short doesn't say anything but he moves over to make room. We all pull together. I feel something give, and the rope comes up and we're all on our backs in the garbage.

Seagulls floating overhead. How do they do that.

We've pulled up an ugly green thing on the end of the rope. Twisted slimy metal. Heavy. Short can barely lift it.

"What is it?" asks Colin.

"That's an anchor, you idiot. Those hook things were caught on something here. Got to be worth twenty bucks to us. I saw a smaller one in Jeb's window marked ninety-five."

Why would anyone throw out an anchor. Mind you, I can't see why anyone would pay ninety-five dollars for one.

"Let's get back to the squat," says Short.

Colin picks up the little brass trophy — a guy bending over, one hand in front like he's feeding ducks, the other behind. I can't figure out what he's doing. Can I go with you guys, I say to Short. Colin is the nice one but Short is the boss.

"He did help us pull it out," says Colin. "The anchor thing." Short turns around. The anchor's too big for him.

I'll carry that, I say.

He frowns. "You got anything on you besides that sheet?" I shake my head.

"Money, a stash, clothes, a place to go?"

Everything I had got burnt or buried, I say.

"Shit, you might as well be a ghost, at that. Here."

I take the anchor. It's slippery and heavy. Colin wraps the sheet around me.

"Just remember," says Short, "you don't get a cut when we sell this."

What does a ghost want with money, I say.

They make anchors heavy — if I were a boat I'd stop. I'm glad Colin and Short don't live far away. We climb through a hole in a fence to a big private lawn with an insane asylum in the background, at least that's what Colin tells me. Through another fence is a bunch of deserted warehouses, big old brick buildings with hooks coming out of them and boards over the windows. No one around. Smell of fish and mud and garbage. Short leads us to the loneliest looking building. One of its bottom windows is missing a board. Short wriggles through, then Colin, then me and my anchor. We're home.

Broken glass everywhere. My feet are numb. I don't know if they were bleeding before but they're bleeding now. I let go the anchor. "Careful," says Short. "The floor's rotten."

I can see us all breathing. No windows or lights, but it isn't dark because there's no roof, just a bank of gray cloud overhead, and a seagull. Nice airy spot, I say. After all, I'm a guest.

"Thanks," says Colin. "We like it." He takes off his dark coat or cape or whatever it is, and hangs it on a nail. Maybe it's a tarpaulin. Green overalls underneath. He bends down and starts puffing at some white coals on a tin tray. When he squats his knees are higher than his ears. He looks like a grasshopper.

Short is standing beside a kid's wagon with rusty wheels. He puts the trophy on it, and some other stuff from his pockets. "Bring the anchor here," he tells me. He keeps his coat on until Colin has a fire going in the tin tray. I pull my sheet around me.

They're burning bits and pieces of driftwood and garbage. It smokes. Good thing there's a draught. Colin puts a can full of water in the fire. Then he goes over to a heap of stuff in the far corner, pulls out a sweater and a pair of pants.

"Hey," says Short. "That's our stuff."

Colin holds up the sweater. "This is too big for you," he says, "and these pants are too big for anybody. With them on he won't look like a ghost." Short subsides.

I'm grateful. The sweater ends at my elbows. The pants end a long way after I do. I'm still grateful. I tuck the pants around my feet, roll the sheet up and sit down on it. Much warmer than the floor. Cold rises out of the ground. They teach you that hot rises, but I've slept out a lot and, believe me, cold rises too.

Short cackles by the fire like an old witch. "You're right," he says. "He don't look like a ghost. He looks like a scarecrow." He goes over to the anchor and cuts some of the rope that's still attached and throws it to me. "Now your pants can stay up," he says.

Colin is stirring the can on the fire. Steam is starting to come out. "Soup's on," he says, taking a cup out of a pocket in his overalls. Short takes a cup out too, and a plastic bag. "You eat out of the can," says Colin.

"When we're finished," says Short.

Gulls overhead all the time. They're much noisier than I

ever thought. Look up and you can see them fighting, scrawing, floating on the air. And they're dirty. The floor is covered in birdshit.

Short takes a handful of green stuff, looks like grass, from the plastic bag, drops some into his cup, some into Colin's, some into the pot. Colin swishes the soup in his cup around, sniffs approvingly. "Good soup today," he says.

"Fresh weeds," says Short. "Picked them yesterday. It makes a difference."

Weed soup. Okay. At least it's hot. And there's more. Colin takes three buns from a shopping bag. Short gets first choice. I don't get a choice. "Don't eat it," Colin advises, "until it's soaked awhile."

"Or you'll lose any teeth you got left." Short opens his mouth wide. His teeth stick out like stumps in cleared ground.

I drop my bun into the can of soup. You guys always eat this good, I say.

"Mostly," says Colin. "The landfill here is the best dump in Etobicoke. And there's a market up on the Lakeshore. Sometimes we get stuff from there, meat and stuff. Remember that stuff we had last week?" Short gives a grunt. He's chewing on his bun.

"We never did decide what it was," Colin tells me. "Might have been fish. Might have been cheese. Might have been bread."

Short shakes his head vigorously. "Wasn't bread," he says.

"Maybe not bread, then. Might have been meat. Except we don't know what kind of meat it could be. It was about this big," he holds his hands out, "and white, and kind of smelly. Not bad, though."

My bun is soft enough to eat now. It doesn't taste like anything.

A gull shits on Colin's head. Short doesn't say anything. Colin rubs his head, goes on eating until his cup is empty. Short puts away his cup, stands up. Colin pats his stomach.

"We should be moving," says Short. "Jeb's place will be open." Colin puts on his coat, or tarpaulin, or whatever it is. The gulls are making a bigger racket than usual. I look up. Fighting over something that's as big as they are. Can it be a fish.

"Come on." Short is standing by the window with the board missing. Colin is pulling the loaded wagon.

I can barely stand up. My feet hurt. They probably hurt before, but I didn't feel it. Now I do. I take a step. I don't know if I can take another one.

Shrieks of rage overhead. A thud on the floor beside me. The gulls have dropped what they were fighting over. Not a fish after all — a boot.

No laces. I don't care. I put it on. It's wet and cold. It doesn't fit. I don't care. It's better than bare skin. I hop-shuffle forward. Let me help you with that, I say to Colin. Together, we lower the wagon to the ground.

Outside the squat is an open area. Used to be for loading and unloading, I guess. Pavement, glass, trash. Some weeds sprouting through the cracks. Short's vegetable garden. My other boot is sitting in the middle of the pavement — it's mine now, anyway.

Colin is pulling the wagon. He looks back to see am I there. Coming, I say.

Clothes on my back. Food in my stomach. Boots on my feet. So much for the outer man. Is it a long way to Jeb's, I say.

"A few blocks," says Colin.

What does he do, I ask him.

Short answers with a grin on his face. "Jeb turns trash into gold."

Lots of opportunity for him hereabouts, I guess.

don't know this part of the Lakeshore Boulevard. The pavement's too wide, the sidewalk's too narrow. Vacant lots, motorcycles, tattoo parlours, table dancers. No one looks at us. Too busy doing not much. The sign over the shop we want is faded and dull. ANTIQUES BOUGHT AND SOLD it says. You can hardly read it. Not that you have to. The front window is full of dusty old stuff. No one's going to mistake the place for the Eaton Centre.

Short opens the door, lets out some dust. The little bell over the door goes *Thuck*. Short coughs, steps inside, calls out, "Jeb?" No answer. We come in with the wagon and stop. There's no room to move, not even to turn around. Things are everywhere, things I know, things I don't know, things nobody could know, all covered in a thick dust icing. Colin coughs. I cough. Short keeps coughing. It's like being inside an old sofa cushion.

"Who's there? And what do you have?" The voice comes from somewhere in the middle of the room. There's a cabinet in the way, with plates that stare at you, and a statue of a frog eating a human leg, a desk with a bagel on top of it, a goose with a light bulb in its mouth. The voice comes from behind all this.

"It's us, Jeb," says Short. "Me and Colin. And we've got some good stuff for you. A fishing net with floats. An anchor and a bowling trophy." He starts to cough again. Jeb doesn't say anything.

"He never comes out," Colin whispers to me. "No one ever sees him."

How long has he been here, I ask.

"I don't know. As long as I can remember." We both start to cough.

"Let me see the stuff," says Jeb. His voice is husky and soft, almost a whisper.

Together, Colin and I lift the anchor. Short holds up the trophy, puts it down and lifts the fishing net. I find myself staring at someone in white glittery clothes, sunglasses and a pompadour. He's holding a microphone. He's almost real size. And he's made out of macaroni.

"Twenty-five," says Jeb.

Short puts down the net. "For what?"

"Everything."

Short looks at Colin, who shrugs. "The anchor's real," says Short. "And heavy. Takes two to lift it. And the other thing is real brass." Jeb doesn't say anything.

"We could go downtown." Short stops to cough. Silence from Jeb. I see a lady with her hands stretched out, beckoning to me. This way, she says. She has long hair and a chipped gold smile. She's beautiful.

"We could go to Church Street." Short makes it sound exotic. Samarkand. Constantinople. "They'd give us more than twenty-five there."

I can't help myself. I drop my end of the anchor and start

towards the lady. She waves her hand, gently encouraging. "Where are you going?" whispers Colin. "Come back." I keep on past tables and stairs, pots and prams and cymbals. I can see her golden lips move. This way, she says to me.

"How about thirty," says Short. "Colin and me, we'd take thirty. Wouldn't we, Colin."

Colin clears his throat. "Sure," he says. "We'd take thirty." And starts to cough.

She's taller than me, the lady with the long hair, and she doesn't have anything on. Her outstretched hand trembles with emotion. I'm almost close enough to touch it.

"Where are you, Mitch?" says Colin. I keep going, reach out my hand and touch — glass. A mirror. I've been running towards a mirror. Where's the lady. I turn around, trying to find her. There's another mirror behind me. With another lady in it. She's still smiling. I blunder about, knocking things over — stuffed animal, ear trumpet, a sailing ship that breaks open to show it's got a bottle inside. Clever. I turn around two or three times. And now my lady's gone. I start to cough. I hear Short's voice.

"Okay," he says. "We'll take twenty-five dollars."

I can't see either of them. I jump up but I can't see over the junk. I try to go back the way I came but I can't remember which way that is. A clock chimes from somewhere. Four strokes. It doesn't mean much. Clocks have been going off since we arrived. I can see three of them and they all show different times.

richard scrimger

160

I hear a cash register. Short's getting his twenty-five. Hey, I say. Hey guys, wait for me. I pick up the pieces of the sailing ship. On the front is my golden lady. She's three inches tall.

"Thanks Jeb," says Short. "See you next time." He coughs.

Hey Colin, wait, I shout, but he doesn't wait.

"Bye," he says. He and Short exit together. The bell goes *Thuck* behind them.

Now what, I say aloud. But Jeb doesn't answer. I cry for help. I cough. I try to find my way out. I cough some more. I walk around and around until I get tired. I wait.

People come into the place, buyers, sellers, traders, Federal Express. I hear them come in. I hear them leave. A mister buys a cane with a pen inside, a lady sells something in a small box. Her soul, she says, she'd give her soul to keep what's in the box. Jeb doesn't want her soul. I try to move in the direction of the voices, but my way is always blocked. I shout and break things but no one pays any attention. Maybe they don't hear me, maybe they've heard it all before. Jeb does business with them and they go out through the door. *Thuck.*

Along the way I find a dark suit. It fits better than my sweater and pants. I find a topcoat too. I never see Jeb or hear him move. I wait.

One guy walks in with a saxophone, walks out humming. Self-sufficient. Another guy buys a ball and chain, for a friend, he says. I find a pair of laces in an ashtray. I put the laces in my boots. I'm all ready to go, only I can't. There's a mirror up ahead, a square one. I take a look at myself. At first I can't tell if I'm an undertaker or someone he's working on. Then I notice that from where I'm standing the mirror reflects the front part of the shop where I came in with Colin and Short. I stare. I've never been this close.

Thuck. A lady walks in slowly. Not young, not well-dressed, not clean. She peers around, coughs, and asks, "Do you have an inexpensive white cane?" Why, I wonder. She can see. Her eyeglasses are the best thing she has on, maybe the best thing she owns.

"Yes," says Jeb.

"Then I wonder if I might offer you my glasses." She fumbles at her face, takes them off. "The frames are solid gold. Eighteen carat. They were bought many years ago. They must be worth a lot of money." She holds up the glasses without being asked. She's been here before. "I've nothing left," she says. "And I'm very hungry. I'd be willing to trade my eyesight for food, only I'd need a white cane to get around. I thought we might strike a bargain."

"Fifty," says Jeb.

The old lady's eyes gleam for a second. "Thank you," she says quietly.

I'm trying to figure out which way the mirror is reflecting. I put my face right up against it, but now it doesn't reflect anymore. It's not a mirror but a window. I'm staring right into the front of the shop. Just a sheet of glass between me and the street door. I think about breaking the glass. I step back to find a hammer or something, and I see that the window is part of a door frame. A complete door and frame standing in the middle of Jeb's shop, hinges, handle and all. People will buy the strangest things. I wonder if the door opens. I take a deep breath and try the handle. It opens. I walk forward, coughing.

The old lady is counting her money. Her glasses are gone. She holds the bills right up to her face. She ignores me. "But where is my cane?" she asks.

"Five for the cane," says Jeb.

"I thought we had a deal."

"Five for the cane."

I step over to the old lady. I'll show you around, I say. Five's a lot of money for a cane. Maybe we can find a cheaper one on Church Street, I say. She tucks her arm in mine.

On the street she takes charge. "Come with me," she says. "Let's celebrate."

Two streets over is a liquor store. They know her there. "Hi, Brian," she says to the guy stacking the red wine.

"Hi, Maisie." He hands her a litre bottle without being asked. Doesn't look at me even though I'm still holding onto her arm.

She says hi to the guy at the cash register too, and hands him a five, about right for a litre. She gets change. "I always drink red," she tells me. "You don't get the same kick from white."

Where to now, I ask.

"Home," she says. "Got to drink the stuff, don't we."

Maisie lives nearby in a real place, with neighbours and mailboxes and an elevator. She says hello to some neighbours, finds a key and opens her door. Inside is a room with a couch and chair. I sit down. She goes into another room, comes back with two tall drinking glasses.

You're not blind, I say.

"That was for Jeb's benefit. Why, you like 'em blind, buddy?" She laughs. "It worked too. I've never heard of anyone getting fifty bucks out of the old miser before." She pours.

Where'd you get the gold glasses, I say.

"They're my mom's." She stops laughing. "Now, drink up."

"Cheryl Ann and I are going horseback riding tomorrow after church." Lucy was carefully casual. "There's a farm outside of Orangeville where I used to ride when I was a kid. We thought we'd try a couple of hours' gentle hacking, then come back to the city for a late lunch and maybe a movie."

Lucy and I were sitting out on the back porch on a summer Saturday evening. I'd spent the day at my desk at the hospital, and there was still a stack of paper to get through before Monday's board meeting. I seemed to be busier than ever, busy even for a doctor. Lucy's Sunday sounded like more fun than mine. I said so.

"Does it? Then, Mitch, why don't you come too?" I stared at her. "If your schedule will let you."

The hospital was sponsoring a new outreach clinic in the West End. I had committed a substantial amount of my time to it, but I found myself saying, I'd love to come.

"Good for you. 'A doctor who is only a doctor is making himself ill, and that is bad practice.'" She was quoting someone. I must have looked blank.

"You said that." When, I wondered. It was true, of course, but most doctors I knew were guilty of it. "Why do you think I love you so much, darling? When you're not fooling yourself you're a pretty smart guy."

No point in quarrelling with a compliment. I leaned back in my chair. A benevolent twilight had smoothed out the hummocks in our back lawn and hidden the bare patches in shadow. A bat swooped out of the foliage overhead. I saw it for a second against the soft purple sky and then it was gone.

"Oh, hi daddy." Cheryl Ann came out to give me a kiss. "I didn't know you were home already. Mummy, guess what, he can come tomorrow. I just talked to him on the phone."

"That's nice, dear." Who can come, I said.

"He knows all about riding, too. He said so." Who, I said.

"I told him just what you said, mummy. He'll be waiting for us at his place at 10:30."

"Fine. I asked your father along. Is that okay?"

Cheryl Ann's grin was sudden and immense, a tropical sunrise. "Yahoo," she shrieked. "Wait'll I tell Leon." She ran inside.

Lucy answered my unspoken question. "Leon Opara, yes. He's been calling here on long weekends and whenever he gets expelled from school. That's every few months or so. He took Cheryl Ann to a dance last week. Didn't you know? He showed up with a limousine and a big bouquet. Didn't you notice the flowers all over the living room?"

How much hadn't I noticed. My memories of Cheryl Ann growing up are fragmented, full of quick cuts. I remember the two o'clock feeds — some of them, anyway. And new shoes and tricycles and the first loose tooth. And the Hallowe'en when she dressed up as a witch and her best friend dressed up as a witch and they met halfway down our street and scared each other to death. Her sneezing fit at my mother's funeral, when the priest swung his censer right in front of us. And I remember always holding hands on the way to the Christmas tree lot, noticing, as the years passed, how her hand grew larger and more confident in mine, until, by the time she was fifteen or sixteen, it seemed that she was leading me along, exhorting, cajoling, promising, as I had done to her when she was small. She couldn't have been more than sixteen. I know that.

That's a father's experience, life in sharp flashes of memory, a highlight film full of touchdowns and interceptions, fumbles, blocked kicks, brilliant open-field running. Champagne for the winners, handshakes and next year for the losers. Life as the fan sees it. Mothers see the whole game, whistle to whistle. They're down there at field level, with the mud and the sweat and the endless third down and five. Life's victories are precious, hard won, infinitely savoured; the losses are agonizing.

And yet I really loved Cheryl Ann, and sometimes it seemed she loved me too. When I quit smoking in the house she used to follow me outside, even if it was raining and we just went to the garage. Lucy's mom, probably just to annoy Lucy, used to call Cheryl Ann a real daddy's girl. Once I asked Lucy if she minded. She shook her head calmly. "It's nice she has a dad to have fun with. You're a treat for her, like chocolate cake. I can't deprive my daughter of chocolate cake."

Oh, I said. What struck me was the absence of jealousy in her voice. Her daughter's love for her wasn't a treat but a fact, calm and unalterable as the times table. Oh, I said, and realized that I was the jealous one. Am I chocolate cake for you too, I asked.

"Oh no. You're the whole meal, cheese dip through to coffee." She smiled. "Only sometimes I feel that the portions could be bigger. I feel like I'm on a diet."

Early services at the United Church on Roncesvalles were given by an old minister with a cane and squint. His sermon was drawn from one of the obscure Old Testament texts, where the prophet Nahum compares the sins of the people to the hairs on the back of a bullock, and their right deeds to the horns of the bullock; and God is the Whip Wielder and the Road Maker, and the way of the prophets is hard, and they are run over by the bullock cart. Or something. At the end he blessed us with a placid smile and told us to go out and have ourselves a nice day.

And we did. We drove up Weston Road and along Lawrence Avenue with the windows down and the radio tuned to Cheryl Ann's favourite station. We played games: animal vegetable mineral, and the game where you add letters to make a word but you're not allowed to finish it. I lost every time and the other two laughed and laughed. The mansions of Post Road came too soon; I'd have driven for hours like that. "Leon's place is the next on the left," said Cheryl, leaning forward in her seat. She smelled nice, I noticed for the first time. Fathers. I caught

Lucy's eye as I slowed and signalled. She smiled.

Leon was waiting for us by the electric gate. He seemed a little nervous, as if he didn't quite belong in the richest square mile of the city. "Hi, Cheri," he mumbled, settling beside her in the back. "Hello, Doctor Mitchell, Mrs Mitchell." I tried not to betray my surprise. Could the Leon I knew have become a shy, polite teenager. "Geez, Mrs Mitchell, I thought you'd drive us in your BMW. This piece of Detroit junk won't even be able to get out of its own way."

Apparently not.

He couldn't break the day for me, I was having too much fun. But he bent it for a lot of others. He bullied the people at the stable, the restaurant and the movie theatre. I didn't think you could bully a popcorn vendor, but he did it. He didn't bully his horse, in fact, he treated it so gently I found myself envying the beast. And he didn't bully Cheryl Ann. He applauded when she attempted a jump and sprang to help her when she fell. And when she passed him the bread basket at the restaurant he said quite distinctly, "Thank you." Then he threw a cherry tomato at the waiter.

What was the attraction, I wanted to know. What did she see in him. It's not perverse, is it, I asked Lucy. We were back at the Oparas' gate, waiting politely and trying not to stare as they said their goodbyes, walking hand in hand under the floodlights.

Lucy laughed. "Some of the best thoroughbreds have a real mean streak. Doesn't mean they're not worth riding. Or betting on."

Lucy fell off her horse. Actually, we all fell, even Leon, and I enjoyed his discomfiture, but Lucy had one very awkward landing on a pile of stones. She was up at once, cursing as she tried to climb back into the saddle, but she favoured her back all evening long and in the morning she couldn't move without pain.

She didn't want to see anyone. I insisted, took her to an orthopædic specialist who shook his venerable head and prescribed rest and painkillers. Lucy thanked him with a grimace and hobbled through his waiting room, which was filled, I noticed, with faces as twisted as hers.

Moira Kilbride, dropping by the house with chocolates and sympathy, suggested alternative therapy. "Why not let Bruno have a go — he's my backtwister. He's got a great grip, Luce. You'll think you're being pulled apart."

Some of my patients went to chiropractors, but I'd never felt comfortable recommending one. Call it snobbery, professional prejudice. An orthopædic surgeon from Johns Hopkins had spent half a drunken hour at a party telling me why, scientifically, chiropractors couldn't do the body any good. "But it's surprising how often the bastards get results. D'you know what it is, Mitchell?" he said, finishing the drink in his hand. "The patients want it to work. They don't like surgery. They don't want to hear me talk about cerebro-spinal fluid and disc degeneration. They want simple solutions, a crack here, a pop there. They're not better, Mitch, they just feel better." And he'd stumped off to the bar.

Moira's backtwister had a respectable address on St George, near the Medical Arts Building. Lucy decided to try him. I couldn't get free so Moira drove her to the clinic. They didn't get home until nearly nine, giggling like mad as they tripped over the doorstep. Cheryl Ann was at a party and I was by myself. I kept expecting to hear Lucy's voice, or to come upon her in the next room. I was so relieved to have her back that I didn't notice right away what the matter was.

Lie down, lie down, I said. Did you hurt yourself again, darling. Moira, are you hurt too, I asked. She was swaying in the doorway.

"I'm fine, mate. We're both fine. Say, is there a tennis racket in the house?"

Lucy twisted around and sat up on the couch. Her hair was in her eyes. "Yes, Mitchell, would you get our rackets. I promised to show Moira how to serve properly. Would you believe she throws the ball in front of her."

I saw now. You've had something to drink, haven't you, I said.

"Yes, dear. Abida insisted, and I didn't like to refuse —"

How's your back. What did the chiropractor tell you.

Lucy smiled. "I feel great."

I rather gathered that, I said with a smile. But what did Dr Laurendeau say. What did he do to you. Lucy, Lu —

She was asleep on the couch, snoring lightly

I stared at Moira. Can I get you a drink, I asked her.

Her laugh sounded like splitting teak. "Thought you'd never ask."

They'd spent the last four hours with Abida, the tennis star. "She sees a chiropractor after every bloody match, even a charity match like the one here; the woman must have a back like bloody Indiarubber," said Moira. "She's from Australia, so when she heard me in the waiting room she introduced herself. After five minutes we were all old friends. Lucy and Abida talked all afternoon, while these stuffed-shirt organizers from the United Appeal hovered around looking at their watches and saying, Oh shit."

They'd gone to dinner, drunk bottles of wine, exchanged phone numbers. They were going to play tennis together as soon as Lucy's back was better. "And that won't be long — just one visit and Lucy was tossing bloody champagne corks in the air, showing off her serve. I thought Abida would bust a gut laughing." Moira banged down her glass, hoisted herself out of the chair and made for the door. Are you all right to drive, I said.

"What the bloody hell d'you mean? I'm from Melbourne."

Cheryl Ann had a funny expression on her face when she came home. "Dad, what's going on? Why is mom sleeping on the couch?"

I'd been afraid to move Lucy in case I injured her again. It's therapeutic, I said. Backs are tricky things.

"Does Auntie Moira have a sore back too? Her car's in the driveway and she's asleep in the front seat."

Abida's invitation arrived a few weeks later on a big thick piece of card with cut edges. She was launching her own line of sportswear. Our presence was requested at the gala, which was being held in the Canadian Room of the Royal York Hotel. At the bottom Abida had written, "So looking forward to seeing you again, Lucy. Hope your first serve is as good as you say."

I straightened my bow tie in Lucy's dressing mirror. We have to leave soon, I reminded her. She was wearing a bathrobe and an expression of distilled concentration. She didn't answer. I went downstairs. Cheryl Ann was teaching herself gin rummy out of a book. There were cards spread out all over the kitchen table. Red jack on the black queen, I suggested. She ignored me. Lucy joined us in a swirling, low-cut dress I'd never seen before. Wow, look at you, I said. Doesn't mom look nice, Cheryl Ann.

"Uh huh." She was sulking. She wanted to come to the party too. "Good night, guys. I hope you enjoy yourselves."

"Good night, dear," said Lucy. Good night, I said, bending to kiss the top of her head.

"Gin," said Cheryl Ann.

In the car Lucy worried that her dress was too revealing. "Abida told me that I should be proud of my body," she said, "but I don't want to be outrageous."

She needn't have worried. Half the women there looked outrageous. Thank heavens for Moira Kilbride's sensible jacket and pantsuit that four bullfighters could have fit into. Lucy attracted her share of appraising glances. No one seemed to care who I was or what I looked like. Certainly not Abida, who greeted me with all the warmth of a car computer telling me that a door was ajar. She took Lucy in her arms.

"You look marvellous," she said.

"So do you," said Lucy. Abida was wearing a man's dinner jacket made of gold-coloured silk. She shook her head. Her hair was improbably red and impossibly long.

"I wear this stuff because of my figure," she said. "If I had your bust I'd flaunt it in a dress like that one." She laughed. The women around her laughed. Lucy blushed. Moira wandered off in search of the bar. I looked at the floor and cleared my throat. When I turned back, Lucy was being introduced to another circle. Someone said something in her ear, took her arm and led her away. She looked over her shoulder at me, helpless, amused, flattered. A waitress came up to me with a tray of glasses. I was alone in the middle of a crowded room with plenty to drink and no one to talk to. Of course, there are worse fates.

That's when I saw her. At first I didn't recognize her. The picture I carried around in my mind was of a different person. This one was taller, fuller, darker in colouring, her hair in a stylish and expensive sweep, clothes only slightly less flamboyant than Lucy's and much more confidently worn, professional makeup, and jewellery. Well well. The old Magda was young enough to be my daughter. For some reason, this one wasn't.

Magda Opara, I said, walking up to her. Nice to see you. Can I get you a drink. She shook her head.

"Not Opara," she said. "These days I go by Magda O'Neill."

Well, of course a lot can happen in, what was it, sixteen years. Congratulations, I said. I didn't know you were married. Is your husband here.

"I'm not married." Her voice was fuller too, and deeper. Then I remembered that O'Neill was her mother's name, the name we'd put on the hospital records. Oh, I said inadequately.

"You're still married, aren't you. I read about you in a magazine a while back. Establishment wife, expensive suite of offices, *Who's Who* client list. And you're on the hospital board, aren't you. I'm impressed, doctor. Between you and my father, you've turned into a success."

I tried to smile. I was having difficulty relating this superbly sophisticated creature to the fifteen-year-old wretch in my memory. A model, dressed in what I presumed was Abida's sportswear, wandered by, hands on hips, smiling glassily. Magda looked her over critically and nodded. The model wandered away. It was the third or fourth time this had happened. What about you, I said. Are you a success too.

"I own an agency now. Offices here and in New York. Those are my people you see wandering around with tennis rackets." She stuck out her chin. "Daddy's money got me started but I'm keeping myself going. Just like you." There was a pleasant hint of mockery in her smile. I found myself liking her.

That's great, I said.

"Isn't it? We'll probably have to expand again. I hate the West Coast, but Lizzie says there's too much business out there to ignore the place entirely." A photographer wanted me to move out of the way so she could take Magda's picture.

Certainly, I said.

For some reason the evening's atmosphere reminded me of my office even though the sounds and smells were different, as was the lighting. Then it hit me. Women. The place was full of women. You can always tell a gynecologist's waiting room from a cardiologist's.

The photographer was asking about "your Lizzie." "She's with the client," Magda said with a professional smile. "Must keep the client happy." The photographer took another shot and left.

Lizzie is your partner, I said.

"Why, yes." She cleared her throat. "Yes, she is. She's known Abida for years. That's how we got the contract. Damn! I thought I had my cigarettes." I offered her one of mine. We smoked companionably for a few minutes.

"Mitch, darling — there you are." Lucy's cheeks were flushed and her hair was coming undone. Magda stared at her.

How are you, dear, I said, taking her hands. Let me present Magda O'Neill. My wife, Lucy.

"Your wife?" Magda sounded like she didn't believe me.

"So it's you we have to thank for these gorgeous models," Lucy said. "I've just been hearing all about you from Elizabeth."

"Oh?"

"She can't stop talking about you."

"Really?"

"She says you're just the greatest thing that's ever happened to her."

Magda's face split into a wide smile. I'd never seen her that happy. *"Really?"*

wake up in blazing afternoon sunlight with a red-wine head. Sharp pain, like knives, right here in the front, spreading down the side like blood dripping. I haven't felt that way in a while. Nostalgia. And I have to go to the bathroom. I get up from the couch and try to find it.

It's not a big apartment. The bathroom won't be far away. Not the room with the stove. Not the room with the body on the bed. Not the closet. Here we are. American Standard. Better now.

Coming out of the bathroom, the kitchen is on my left, bedroom on my right, living room in front of me. Maisie's on her feet in the living room. That's her name, Maisie. "Out of the way, buddy," she says. "I feel like I swallowed a lizard."

I go into the bedroom. The body belongs to a very old lady with wispy hair. Her housecoat is striped. Her skin is white. Dead white. That's where they get it. I touch her. Cold. I go back to the living room. Is the bottle empty, I wonder. Yes it is. When Maisie gets back I ask, Who is the dead body.

"Mom," she says. "Who else?"

Of course, I forgot. The lady with the golden glasses.

"She died the other day, just went to bed and didn't get up in the morning. It was a Tuesday, I think, because I heard the radio next door when I got up. Tuesday. And today is Wednesday. Isn't it?"

She's asking the wrong person. I nod, but I'm just being polite.

"She was breathing kind of funny before she went to bed. Sharp and gasping. I thought about taking her to the clinic, but I decided to wait and see how she was in the morning. And in the morning she was dead. I've known her all my life and now she's dead. There isn't anyone else I've known all my life."

I don't know what to do. I put my arm around Maisie.

"All that day I watched her. I kept expecting her to move, but she didn't. Her glasses were on the bedside table. I thought about putting them on her, but her eyes were closed. And I was afraid to touch her. I still am. I went outside and wandered around, and then I found myself at Jeb's. I still had her glasses in my hand. So I put them on."

I feel uncomfortable standing there. I sit Maisie down and sit beside her. Now it's a comedy. You have to get a doctor, I say.

"I don't know a doctor except at the clinic. And what can a doctor do?"

A doctor can say she's dead, I say.

"Shit. I can say she's dead. She's got flies crawling on her, she hasn't breathed in days. A fucking moron can say she's dead." Maisie's right of course. And she's getting upset again.

What do you want, I say.

"I want her back. And since I can't have her back, I want her gone. Now, today. I want to go into the bedroom and not find her there. Listen," she says. "You can help me. Why don't you get rid of her. Would you do that for me? I'd do it myself, but I can't touch her."

I swallow. I wish the bottle wasn't empty.

"I know it's a lot to ask," she says, pulling at my sleeve, "but I can't stand the thought of her being here another day. I know what'll happen if I go to the clinic. They'll ask questions about how she died and when she died and what happened to her glasses — and I won't be able to tell them. And I'll feel stupid. It'll be so much easier if you'd just take the body someplace and let them find her. I mean it. I'll get you some more to drink," she says. "I'll pay you. I got that money from Jeb. I'll give you some of it. I'll give you half of it. I'll do anything. Only get her out of here."

And she starts to cry. I'm holding her, and she's crying, with her face screwed up like a used dishcloth. Not a big healthy boo hoo, but a weak gasping sound, like a cat being sick.

I'm afraid of that sound. Babies make that sound when they've failed the APIT test and gone into respiratory distress. You've got to act fast, brain damage can occur within a few minutes — oxygen, fibrillation, there isn't much time. I force Maisie's head back, open her mouth and breathe into it. Come on, I say, pushing her down onto the couch, trying to inflate her lungs artificially.

She draws her arms around me and sticks her tongue in my mouth. No no, I say. You've got to breathe. My face is right up to hers. She isn't crying any more. She's breathing fine. She pulls me down on top of her. For an older lady she's pretty strong.

Her neck is dirty. She tastes of vomit and red wine. "I want you," she says in my ear. Oh my. Her dress has more buttons than my shirt. Her brassiere is beige — or at least it's beige now. Underneath it her breasts are beige too, with a surprising ring of dark hair surrounding the sunken nipples like a what is it, a tonsure. One of the aureoles is off centre. It doesn't react like the other one when I use my mouth and fingers. The nipple doesn't erect. There's a small lump behind it, shouldn't be there. She scratches my chest. Her fingernails are long. It doesn't hurt. She laughs in her throat.

I try to stand up but her hands are everywhere. Now she's on top of me, shaking her breasts in my face. She crawls down me, undoes my new pants and reaches inside. She uses her fingernails again. It still doesn't hurt. Not at all. I'm surprised at myself. I can't remember the last time I had an erection. Maisie bends down to kiss the top of it. Then she takes out her false teeth seductively. "You'll like this," she mumbles, tossing the teeth aside and bending down again. And you know, I do. The couch is uncomfortable but I hardly notice.

Dead people stink. In the spring you find them in the park under the leaves. It's always surprising. Not roses. And dead people don't fit. Wherever you want to put them, they want to go someplace else. Maisie's mom is about five feet — well, she's not tall any more, say five feet long — and skinny, but I can't get her into the bundle buggy.

I don't know why I'm doing this. I'm pretty sure it's wrong. Stupid too. But it's what Maisie wants. She won't help, won't even watch. And she's impatient. "Are you ready yet?" she snaps from the living room — her teeth are back in. Not yet, I say.

Daylight fades from the bedroom, filling it with shadows. Flies hover and settle. I don't even want to think about what's going on inside Maisie's mom. I've got her wrapped in a coat, but it keeps coming undone and bits of her show through. My hands are sweaty, sliding over toes and ankles. Hard to get any leverage. Sorry, I say to her. I don't know any name for her except mom. I give a last push and she collapses like a lawn chair, knees under her chin. Now I can slide her into the bundle buggy, and she fits, almost. One leg sticks out no matter how hard I shove. Sorry, mom. I tip the buggy upright and cover the leg with a bag from Karl's Sausage Shop. It's not big enough. Do you have a garbage bag, I ask Maisie.

It takes both of us to pull the buggy through the apartment. Maisie keeps her head down. The purse she's carrying bumps against the side of the buggy. She's making a moaning noise, "uuuuuh, uuuuuh." She doesn't know she's doing it. I ask her to stop but she doesn't hear me.

"I can't bear it," she whispers when we get to the hall. "Does it look natural? Like we're going shopping or something?" Sure, I say. I don't know why she's whispering, the hall's empty.

Maisie directs us past the elevator. "The back stairs," she whispers. "Quieter." Okay, I say.

"Will we get away with it?" Her question echoes in the dark stairwell. Sure, I say. Then we lose control of the buggy and it tumbles down two flights making quite a racket. A door opens at the bottom and someone begins to scream. I grab Maisie's arm to pull her back up the stairs, but she can't move. We stand still and and listen. After a moment the screaming stops and the voices begin.

"Must have tumbled down," says more than one.

"Maisie should never have let her — not at her age."

"Call the police. Call the fire department."

"Here's her shopping bag. Groceries must have fallen out."

"The food's nearby. Sausage — sure smells like it."

"Where's Maisie? What a shock this will be for her."

"What a shame." More than one voice says that too.

Carefully we tiptoe back up to Maisie's floor and take the elevator down. We don't see any neighbours. On the street Maisie starts giggling, can't stop. "They all think she fell," she says. "When I get back she'll be gone! The ambulance will come to take her away and she'll be gone! Mama, oh mama!" Then she starts to cry. Hysteria. I pat her arm, pull her along. There's a place with flashing lights up ahead. Is it a bar.

She sniffs, wipes her face with her bare hand, sniffs some more. That's better, I say.

I was right, the flashing light is a bar. Maisie keeps going. "Not there," she says. "I always go there. I want to go someplace different. Besides, it's the first place they'll look for me." I guess she's right. She isn't crying any more. Her cheeks are smeared from where she rubbed her tears away. I can see what she looked like when she was a little girl.

"There are other bars," she says.

Do I know this part of town. It's oddly familiar. Every now and then I can smell the waterfront. Seagulls scramble for food in a parking lot. We turn another corner and we're back on the Lakeshore Boulevard. The streets aren't numbers anymore. Now they're bodies of water, Pacific, Superior. Didn't that place on the corner used to be a bar, I say.

"Oh, sure. Long John Silver's. But that was ten or fifteen years ago. It's been a lot of things since then." It's for rent now.

I stop dead in the middle of a driveway. I know where I am. PRIVATE PARKING. AUTHORIZED VEHICLES ONLY. A small sign on the wall, with rude instructions spray-painted around it. Disrespectful. I remember the sign. This is the clinic, I say.

Maisie starts, like she's been asleep. "My God, so it is. I didn't mean to come this way. I've been here so often with mom, I guess I wasn't thinking where I was going."

An old guy is crossing the road in front of an ambulance. The siren cuts in to tell him to hurry up. He stops. The ambulance pulls around him, screeches to a stop beside the clinic door. Maisie clutches my arm. "Is that mom?" she whispers.

No, I say. The ambulance driver runs to open the back door. There's no hurry for your mom.

Maisie shudders. "I need a drink."

There's a bar on the next block. Plants in the window, soft music, darts. We don't belong. We're the only ones there, but we don't belong. "Vodka," says Maisie to the girl behind the bar. "Double." The girl is staring at me like I've just come out of the ground. I put on my best smile. "Give him the same," says Maisie. She throws down a bill. Thanks, I say.

An hour later the place is still empty. The girl behind the bar is saying, "Anything else?" hoping we'll say no. I'm yawning. The room is getting soft and fuzzy at the edges. Either it's full of cotton wool or I am.

"Another round," says Maisie.

t was April, soft showers and spring flowers like they say, only I was inside. The lights were on, the jackets were off and the Chairman of the Board of Directors was announcing the last item on the agenda. "The Civic Hospital's Western Outreach Clinic will open officially this Thursday," he said with pride. "You will recall that my predecessor in the chair laid the foundation stone two years ago. I have arranged for a plaque bearing the names of this Board of Directors to be erected in a suitable spot." A hum of approval circulated around the table like an expensive bottle of port. There we were, doing good and getting credit. "I understand," here the chairman looked down the table at me, "that the Chiefs of Surgery, Medicine and Obstetrics will themselves be taking part in the day-to-day functioning of the new clinic. Isn't that so, Dr Mitchell?"

I nodded gravely. We thought, Mr Chairman, that senior staff participation would be an indication of our commitment to the new clinic, I said.

More approval. Discreet applause. Amazing how easy it is to sound pompous. I thought back to the senior staff discussion in Ray Lieberman's office. Most of the time had been spent worrying about reserved parking.

After board meetings we always had a few minutes of

coffee chat. "I'm glad you're going to be part of the clinic team, Mitchell," said the chairman. "It means a lot to the hospital. Makes us look good. I know it's a sacrifice for you, but the timing may work out very well. I got a call from *Maclean's* over the weekend. They're doing a feature on outreach medicine. Your name came up in our discussion." I murmured something appropriate. He smiled. "I won't say more than that now. Oh, and I'm sorry that Leon wasn't feeling well enough to attend this morning. We all missed him, of course. Would you please convey my personal best wishes for a speedy recovery the next time you see him?"

As it happened I was seeing Opara for lunch that day. We often lunched on Mondays. His gout was acting up, so we ate at the house instead of his favourite restaurant. I mentioned the chairman's best wishes.

"Damned old boot licker," Opara snorted, which was unfair. The chairman wasn't more than fifty. "He knows I think the clinic is a waste of time and money, but his chair's up for renewal and he wants my vote." I was puzzled. Won't *Maclean's* be good for the clinic and the hospital in the long run, I said.

"National exposure won't help a local hospital pay its bills. To most people outreach clinics mean gunshot wounds, venereal disease and pregnant teenagers. Who's going to write a cheque for that?" He went back to his grapefruit.

But how important is it for a hospital to pay its way, I said. He stared at me. He was a prominent philanthropist, gave away more in a year than I'd ever earn, but he looked at me with a disgust you only see on school playgrounds. Forget it, I said. When the servant brought my cheese he took some too. Is that on your recommended diet, I asked.

"Of course not." He took a bite. "But I like cheese. I don't actually like too many things." Each to his gout, I said.

"You know who else likes cheese? Not this Cheshire, either, but the real rich stuff? Your daughter. Young Leon brought her over for dinner the other evening. He's, um, home from Benson-hurst." Opara coughed. I took it that Leon had been expelled again. "And young Cheri — that right?"

Cheryl Ann, I said.

"He called her Cheri. Anyway, she had three pieces of Stilton after dinner and dessert. Healthy appetite. I like to see that in a girl. I took quite a liking to her. She's got a lot of spunk for a doctor's daughter, ha ha." I laughed too.

"I hope," he went on more quietly, "that she doesn't take Leon too seriously. They're both young, of course."

I frowned. Was he suggesting that Cheryl Ann wasn't good enough for his grandson. What are you getting at, Opara, I said.

He stared at the table. "This is hard for me," he said. "Young Leon is a bit wild right now. I'll be sending him to a military academy next term. Maybe they'll be able to force some discipline down him. The other night at dinner I was uneasy, watching him and your daughter together. The teenage years are tough for everyone. She's um, smaller than he is. I wouldn't want her to get hurt." I swallowed. I couldn't say anything. "I wouldn't want him to hurt her," he said at length, without looking up from his plate. And I saw that he was ashamed.

I think we were both relieved when my beeper went off. Mrs Nokes, a jolly, dishevelled woman with a penchant for ugly jewellery, was about to have her seventh child. At forty-five, too.

Are you sure you want the baby, I'd asked, because at your age I'm sure —

"Don't ask me," she'd said. "Ask *her*." All Mrs Nokes' babies were *her* until they were born. "I'll just be bringing her up. It's her you'll be cutting off before her prime."

I liked Mrs Nokes. This was our fifth go-round. She never got to the hospital with more than an hour to spare. I had to hurry.

And that's final, I said, like a cartoon father. Cheryl Ann giggled. I mean it, I said. He's not to come here. You're not to see him.

"Daddy, you make him sound like a vampire."

"Darling, your father is just worried about you." Lucy had her arm round the girl's shoulders. She shook her head at me. They seemed to be on the same side. I didn't understand.

What is the problem here, I said. I know for a fact that the boy you are seeing is violent and dangerous. His own guardian and grandfather —

"That sweet old geezer."

Yes, that sweet old geezer, I said with an involuntary smile, told me himself that he was worried about Leon hurting you.

"Has he ever done anything like that?" Lucy asked.

"Of course not!"

Have you ever seen him angry, I asked.

"Sure. Lots of times. But I can handle him." This sounded like every victim of domestic violence I'd ever heard of. I looked to Lucy for support. She patted Cheryl Ann on the shoulder.

"When is he going away to the military school?"

"Next week," said Cheryl Ann. "He'll be gone for the rest of the term. Unless he's kicked out," she added hopefully.

"Let's think about this," said Lucy. What is there to think about, I wondered. "A few months — that's not very long, is it. It'll pass in no time, darling."

Will it, I said.

"I don't know," said Cheryl Ann.

"And a little while apart will give you two a chance to find out how much you mean to each other. It's really a very civilized arrangement," said Lucy.

"I guess." Cheryl Ann slouched up the stairs. "I'll phone him now. Can I invite him for dinner tomorrow?"

"Of course." Lucy watched her go affectionately. Then she turned. "You idiot!" she said, and the glory and wonder of it all was that she looked at me affectionately too. "Didn't you notice the pendant Cheryl Ann was wearing?" I hadn't, of course. "She told me all about it, it's her first gift from a boy and she had to tell someone, apart from her best friends. He went down on one knee and everything. Isn't it sweet?"

I said the first three things that came into my head. She's too young, I said. No, it isn't sweet. I want a drink.

"I got a fraternity pin when I was about Cheryl Ann's age,

and I didn't tell my mom because I knew she'd take it away from me. I want to give Cheryl a chance to enjoy Leon's attention."

But he's not very nice, I said.

"Who wants a nice boyfriend when you're sixteen? Let her get Leon out of her system now, and in five or ten years she'll marry the nicest man in the world."

What makes you think so, I said.

She took my hand. "I did."

The sight was familiar. I wouldn't claim to be able to recognize all my patients from the waist down, but Mrs Nokes was an old friend. That's fine, I said. Looks great. Six weeks since the baby was born and everything healing nicely. And you've had no fresh bleeding — no bright red.

"No, doctor." A disembodied voice from behind the out-spread thighs.

Good, I said. A few more routine questions finished the examination. I took off my gloves and helped her sit up.

"You know, the older I get, the more awkward that — apparatus seems to be," she said gesturing toward the stirrups. A lot of women say that, I told her.

"Enough to make you think, isn't it, doctor. Or perhaps not. Tell me, have you ever put your own feet in them and tried staying still for fifteen minutes?" I stared at her.

Well, no. I'm a man, I said. I left the cubicle and went across to my desk.

While I wrote up her file, Mrs Nokes asked me about the family. "And your little girl, Cheryl Ann. She'll be sixteen now, won't she." How did Mrs Nokes know that.

Yes, I said. Sixteen last February.

"How the time goes. I remember you telling me about her

first teeth. An Aquarian she is, like our Maureen." I begged Mrs Nokes' pardon.

"February is the Water Bearer's month. Tell me, is she imaginative? Aquarians often are. You should hear Maureen's stories. I don't know where she gets all the stuff in her head."

Mrs Nokes was my second last patient that day. I went with her to the waiting room, where my receptionist, my nurse and a slim version of Mrs Nokes were peering into a well-worn stroller, admiring the baby boy. The girl was a year or two younger than Cheryl Ann. I must have delivered her. I couldn't remember her name.

"Isn't he adorable," Mrs Nokes whispered to me. "The wee little hairless thing. I think he's my favourite." I smiled. Mrs Nokes said that about each new baby.

"Can I push, mom?" asked the girl.

"Course you can, Rosie dear," said Mrs Nokes. "Say goodbye to the doctor, now."

Goodbye, Rosemary, I said. Yes, I'd delivered her. Breech, with one leg twisted around behind her ear. She'd had to wear a brace for a few months.

The senator's wife was late. Mrs Titus O'Neill, now in her fifth month and hoping for a boy to carry on the senator's name, was usually late. But I'd been expecting the wrong O'Neill. My nurse nodded at the seated young woman I should have recognized.

"Ms O'Neill called this morning. She said you'd treated her

before, but I couldn't find a file. I made up a new one. Was that all right?"

I took the crisp patient folder. Hello, Magda, I said.

She looked stunning. I ushered her into my office and closed the door. She gazed around, nodding every now and then. It was a big room, with a bay window overlooking Russell Hill Road. Books, chairs, pictures, panelling. Most of my patients liked it.

"Good," she said softly. "Very good. A room for the successful older man. Your patients come in here and feel safe with daddy." I didn't answer. I wondered why she'd made the appointment. I'd have bet money she wasn't pregnant.

She poked her head into the cubicle. I didn't ask her what she thought of the stirrups. Are you still living in New York, I said. She nodded, very reserved. No, not reserved. Afraid. What's the matter, Magda, I said.

She turned and pointed her chin. "I want you to examine me."

I didn't move. Go on, I said.

"Last week I got a phone call from L.A. We're thinking — we were thinking — of expanding the agency. Lizzie was on the line and she was hysterical. For awhile now she's been having these sudden sharp pains, like bad menstrual cramps; they'd last a few minutes and then go away. She had an attack in L.A., strong enough to send her to hospital. The doctor examined her and made her stay overnight and ran a lot of tests and ... it turns out to be cancer. Fast-growing, past the operable stage. They're going to try some kind of chemotherapy — but without much hope. It's a matter of months, they said. Months. She's thirty years old."

Her breathing was ragged. I came around the desk, pulled up another chair, patted her arm. That's horrible, I said. Horrible and unfair. Meanwhile wondering why she was here. There was more coming.

"I wanted to fly out but her folks are there, they live in L.A., and it would be ... awkward." She took a deep breath. "And then this morning I woke up with these severe pains. I remembered what Lizzie said: like being stuck with poisoned arrows. That's exactly what it felt like. I made the appointment right away and caught the noon flight. Doctor, you must examine me." Turning to grab me by both arms, "You must."

Magda, I said, you know that cancer is not measles. You don't get it from someone else. What happened to Lizzie is tragic, but it doesn't affect your own physical health, I said.

"I know, but —"

And you know I'm an obstetrician, not a cancer specialist. I do some gynecological work, but I'm not the best examiner around. If you're in pain you should certainly see someone, and the sooner the better. Is your own doctor here or New York, I said. Or I could recommend —

"No! It has to be you!" I couldn't understand her vehemence, but I felt it would be wrong to argue further.

I expected to find nothing. I was wrong. You have a Renzler infection, I told her.

"What?" Struggling onto her elbows.

Nothing alarming, people get them all the time, I said. It's like persistent, localized yeast. I'll write you a prescription. Use it twice a day. You want to wash thoroughly and wear cotton underwear. No astringents, no tight pants. The infection should clear up in about a week, I said.

"Oh my God." She started to cry. "I knew it. I knew if I came here it would be all right."

Nothing brilliant about the diagnosis, I said. The infection is unmistakable. Anyone would have spotted it.

"Thank you, thank you. No, don't go, doctor." I'd been about to leave the cubicle while she dressed. "Don't leave me yet." All right, I said. I smiled and turned discreetly away.

You should make another appointment in a week, I said. Here or New York, it doesn't matter. But someone should check to make sure the infection is going away. Will you remember to do that, I said. But she just kept crying and thanking me.

"Isn't that nice," said Lucy when I told her. "To Magda you're a miracle worker. Leon was supposed to die and didn't. If you examine her, she won't have to die either."

Because I'm such a great doctor, I said.

"I don't think it has to do with skill. You're more like a fetish. An amulet. A good luck charm." Oh, I said.

"How horrible about Lizzie. I met her at Abida's clothing launch. A striking girl. She and Abida used to be lovers, I think. I wonder if it made Magda jealous?"

How did she know about Magda. After the examination I'd told her to stay away from sex for a couple of days, and then resume gradually. There may be some residual discomfort, I'd said. You'll want to make sure you're lubricated and, of course, your, uh, partner should use a condom.

Magda had laughed and laughed. "Where should my, uh, partner put the condom, doctor?" Then she'd started to cry. "Oh, my poor Lizzie!"

Sweat all over me when I wake up. I feel red, flushed, like a sanitary napkin in a public bathroom. Magda, I say. Oh God.

"It's Maisie," says the voice beside me. "Try and remember the girl's name. It makes us feel better." Better than what, I wonder. It's dark. No it isn't. Not quite. We're lying on someone's front lawn looking up, at least I am, and a long way off at the edge of the sky is some light. Dawn above me and dew underneath.

"When I was a little girl," says Maisie, "I used to love this time of day. I'd get up and look out the window for the milkman. He'd see me in the window and wave. I used to think he was so handsome in his uniform. His horse was black, I remember." Maisie's dating herself. Our milkman drove a van. "The bottles would clink against our doorstep. And mama would let me have first pour, so I'd get the cream." She sniffs. "Oh mama," and starts to cry. I reach to pat her hand, but she's moved away.

"I have to get home."

I'll go with you, I say.

"No." Very definite. "They'll be waiting for me. The police and the neighbours. I don't want them ... to see ...." She coughs and doesn't finish. Well, I can take a compliment.

Fine, I say. I don't blame you. Thanks for the drinks, I say. See you around sometime.

We're on our feet now, neither of us any too steady. The sky is bright enough to let you know it's going to be a lousy day. Clouds roll by fast and low, bumping into each other. Maisie leans forward like she's about to fall, gives me a peck on the cheek. Her breath is not minty and fresh. "Goodbye," she says, "and thank you for trying to ... for helping with mother." Her blouse hangs open so that I can see the tops of her breasts under her bra. That reminds me.

You know, Maisie, about that breast. You should —

"What are you talking about?" She steps back, covers herself.

You may have a problem, I say.

"You think I'm a slut, is that it? Is that it? You're criticizing me? You think I drink too much and sleep with anybody? That's rich, coming from you."

No, I say.

"Look who's talking. I don't live on the street. I don't piss blood and cry in my sleep. I don't drink a person's booze and then tell them *they* have a problem. Solve your own problems first, buster. Drink and sex aren't going to kill me." She stomps off into the sunrise.

She's probably right too.

I head towards the lake, I think. It's downhill, anyway. After a couple of blocks I run into a crowd of people. I try to go around them but I can't. They fill the sidewalk, spilling into the street with their signs and banners and babies, shouting angry words. They don't look angry, though. They look wet. It's starting to rain. More people arrive in school buses. I try to back away but they're behind me now, pushing me on. I don't know what to do. I keep going.

Lights flash at the edge of the crowd. Police watch, standing beside their cars, arms crossed. Cameras pan back and forth. A loud voice up ahead is bellowing instructions. Stand here, get in line, walk this way. I don't want to. I try to squirm out of the way. I can't. I shut my eyes and go limp. I'm carried along, a twig in a stream. We're on the Lakeshore again, right out in the middle of the street. They've stopped traffic for us. Mimico, they used to call this part. I don't know what they call it now.

Someone hands me a sign. I don't know what to do with it. I hold it up like everybody else. A loud voice tells us to march and we march, and to shout and we shout. I have no idea what we're saying. La la la, I shout. We stop marching in front of a store called SHOP AND SAVE. Used to be an A&P. The noise is louder. We wave our signs and shout. I know where we are. We're opposite the clinic.

The woman in front of me is carrying a baby. She doesn't seem worried about it getting caught in the crush. Other people are carrying babies too. Suddenly I can't breathe. I look up at my sign for the first time and I see it's a picture of a baby lying in a coffin. I drop it like it's burning hot. I turn around, trying to get out get out get out. Someone is standing on the steps of the clinic now, waving a bullhorn, chanting. La la la la, he says. I can't get out. I don't want to hurt the babies but I have to get out. The police look bored. How can they look bored. The crowd waves their signs. I see more pictures — dead babies in coffins, babies on the gallows, in the electric chair, under the guillotine. LEGAL MURDER? say the signs. LEGAL MURDER? I can't take it any more. I fall to my knees and put my hands over my ears. Tears are pouring down my cheeks. The crowd leaves me alone. Maybe they think I'm praying. Maybe I am.

"You okay, buddy?" A gentle voice in my ears. Firm hand on my shoulder. "Let's get you out of here. Can you stand up?" I shake my head, and the hand lifts me up and steers me out of the crowd. It's a cop. I look over in surprise, she smiles at me encouragingly. "Too much for you, eh?" she says. "I was watching you. You look like you need a hand." I'm so sorry, I say.

"No bother." She misunderstands. "Just doing my job." She's looking all around as she leads me away. Crowd control. She's my height and a lot wider, her hip bumps into mine.

No, I'm really sorry, I say. Can you forgive me.

Something in my voice. She stares. Her eyes are small and dark. There's no twinkle in them. "I'll take you back to your bus," she says. She thinks I'm one of the marchers. "Come on. I'm not supposed to leave my post." Strong arms she's got.

There's a whole row of yellow school buses in the lot beside the SHOP AND SAVE. The nearest one has its doors open so the driver can smoke without getting wet. She's leaning in the doorway, relaxed, one hand in her pocket. When she sees us coming she flicks away her cigarette and steps down into the rain. I follow the burning arc. It hits the pavement and bounces into a puddle, leaving behind a dying shower of sparks.

"He's feeling faint," says the cop. The driver nods. She's so young. Even younger than the cop. Got a cap perched on the back of her head. Blonde hair underneath the cap, gray eyes.

"Can't say I blame him. Come on in, then," she says to me. Not a city voice. Too flat, too smooth, too slow. "Thanks, officer," she says, but the cop is already on her way back to the street, head up, eyes ranging, hips swinging.

I stumble on the rubber steps. The way is narrow. I can't get up by myself. The driver guides me into a warm, familiar seat. Rain comes down harder. I can hear it on the roof and windows. "There," she says. "You're all right. You can relax."

I didn't come on the bus, I say.

"That's all right. You sit and rest a while. Are you thirsty?" She goes away, comes back with a thermos and a stack of Dixie cups. And a handkerchief. "Here. You've got a thing hanging from your nose," she says. The handkerchief smells nice. I'm sitting in the same springy seat I had when I was ten years old and on my way to St Anthony's Parish Picnic. I breathe deeply. It always rained on the weekend of the parish picnic.

She sits beside me, pours me some juice without a word. My hand shakes as I take it. I'm sorry, I say. The shouting of the crowd is a long way off. The rain is closer, friendlier.

It was the noise, I say. And the people, all around. And the signs. The pictures. The babies. I'm sorry, so sorry, I say.

"For what — for feeling faint?"

No, I say.

"For what, then?"

For everything, I say.

The bus shifts ever so slightly as someone climbs on. "Katie, have you seen Father Douglas?" A woman's voice. She sounds like the signs outside, loud, upset. She sees me. "And who is that with you?"

The bus driver's name is Katie. It suits her. "Father Douglas left for the press conference," she says. "I'm sitting here with a casualty. Mary Alice, perhaps you — why, what's the matter?"

She's staring at me, a plain middle-aged woman who has suddenly seen a ghost. Thin, severe, earnest, with her mouth screwed up in a little O of pain. I remember someone just like her at my parish picnic. There are some at every parish picnic. "Are you him?" she whispers.

"Mary Alice, is everything all right?" asks Katie.

"No, you can't be him," she says. "You're thinner and almost bald. He had a beard. It's just that for a second I thought you were someone I saw once. Oh, Jesus," she says. "Excuse me, Katie. There's Father Douglas now. I've got to ...." She leaves. Katie looks at Mary Alice, looks at me.

"We're from out of town," she says. "Mary Alice works in the parish. Do you know her?" I shake my head, no.

"She used to work in a parish in Toronto. We're supposed to be nice to her, but sometimes it's hard. She's so angry. She

collects anti-abortion literature and goes to all the meetings.
She's kind of crazy, really. You're sure you don't know her?"

I shake my head. I'm wondering if I can ask about lunch.
Feels like days since I ate last.

Katie tells me not to move, says she'll get me lunch. She smiles as she says this. I wonder how old she is. I hope her father loves her. We eat in the school bus. Everyone is wet and very nice to me, smiling, saying hello before moving to the back. Father Douglas asks how I'm doing, but the beeper in his pocket rings before I can tell him. He's tall dark and busy, he pumps my hand and heads off. "Well done, team!" he calls on his way out the door. He's got a lot to do. Mary Alice gives out the sandwiches. She keeps staring at me. I say, Thank you. She shudders. Good to know I've still got it.

The bus windows are steamed up. I write with my finger, not paying any attention, rubbing out the word when I hear footsteps. I take a sip from my Dixie cup. Katie sits down beside me, gestures at the window.

"I was watching you," she says. "You wrote the word *Home* on the window, and then rubbed it out." Now that the glass is clear I can see the tree outside. They've piled their signs at the bottom of the tree. LEGAL MURDER? I look away.

"Where do you live?" she asks. "Where is home?" I don't say anything. We sit quiet for a bit before she goes on. "The reason I ask is that the bus will be leaving soon. It's at least an hour to Dundurn and we want to beat the rush-hour traffic out of the city. I was wondering if we could give you a lift somewhere. Maybe drive you – home."

I say the first thing that comes into my head.

"I'm sorry," bending closer. "I didn't hear you." I say it again.

"Sunnyside?" she says. "Was that it? Is that where you'd like to go?" I nod. "Do you know where it is? How to get there?"

It's near here, I say. But I don't know where.

Across the aisle is a silvery old woman. I like her. She wouldn't carry a sign, said they were in questionable taste. And she nodded to me when she came in, very friendly. Looked right at me.

"I remember Sunnyside," she quavers.

There's a lot of shushing so she can be heard. "It was an amusement park in the west end of the city, near the National Exhibition grounds. The tram went down Roncesvalles and let you off near the roller coaster. Five cents that tram used to cost, but some of the drivers would let you on for nothing. I think Sunnyside had the first roller coaster in North America, even before the one at Coney Island. And a wide sandy beach where folks used to go swimming and boating. And there was a dance hall too, I'll never forget. The Palais Royale. Why, it was famous. Everybody played there, Harry James, Benny Goodman, Duke Ellington. I got engaged there, back in 1946. My Dave asked me right on the dance floor and the bandleader played that song, 'Congratulations.' We used go down there every chance we could.

"Once Dave got in a real fight because another boy asked

me to dance, and he cut himself and had to be taken up the street to the hospital. Great days they were, heavenly days, with the moon on the water and the band playing and all of us so young and happy." Her eyes mist over like a cold windshield. No one tells her to be quiet. "Sunnyside's not the same now. The amusement park is gone. The Palais Royale is shut. The hospital, St Joseph's, is still there, though. You can see it from the expressway."

Katie is looking at me all this time, at my face and hands. "Thank you, Margaret," she says to the old lady, who's sitting down now, lost in her memories. "We'll try the hospital."

The bus sounds like a beast warming up, an old black-and-yellow tiger that's eaten a bunch of Christians. It lurches forward, shaking the water off its heavy paws, pad pad pad through the traffic jungle. The Lakeshore Boulevard's almost empty. No more people in front of the clinic. No more signs. I see a block of empty storefronts and a strip of warehouses, and motels advertising comfortable beds. We pass by. We're on a low road. Above us loom great arches of concrete with the expressway on top. We keep going down. The road snakes around a bit and soon we're under the concrete arches.

"We're going to have to take a detour," says Katie. "They've closed that stretch of the road. I don't really know where I am. I'm just following the guy ahead of me." Sounds like a good plan to me. The road bends some more. We're not the only ones on it, there's quite a few of us following the guy in front.

richard scrimger

I settle against the springy cushions and wait.

The window keeps getting steamed up. I rub it clean a few times and then give up. Katie can see. It doesn't matter if I can. "Guthrie Avenue. Ringley Avenue. And Park Lawn Road. Darn." Katie shakes her head. I clean my window. Little empty streets. There's no one ahead of us now. No one to follow.

"This is no good," she says. "We're just going in circles. Every road in this part of the city is under construction. How many times have we been on Park Lawn."

The bus is full of uneasy muttering. They're talking about me. These nice friendly folks with their prayers and sandwiches all want to get rid of me. I know the tone of voice. I've heard it before. They're in a hurry to get away from me. They want to toss me overboard like that poor guy with all the bad luck. What was his name. And the damn crocodile waiting for him, tick tock.

Katie makes a left turn onto a busy street, pulls the bus over onto the shoulder. Outside my window is a high barbed-wire fence. Behind it, a parking lot full of huge trucks. Away in the distance the traffic floats down the expressway like so much timber to be pulped. My window begins to get foggy again.

Katie comes over to sit next to me. "It's after five o'clock," she says. "I'm afraid we're not going to be able to take you home tonight." I stare out the front window. Cars are crawling past us. Lots of cars on this street. Only one lane is working, but it's working hard.

"The roads are all being torn up, and we're running out of time. I have to drive these people back to Dundurn. They have homes too. Do you understand?" I nod.

"Do you?" She's very serious. Her hand is on my arm. She wants me to tell her it's okay.

Sure, I say. I get up. Thanks, I say to everyone. And then, to her, Thanks Katie.

She walks me to the door and helps me down. It's a damp evening, not quite raining. "That's the way you want to go," she says, pointing ahead. "The road is closed to traffic but I've seen people walking."

I stand there while she backs the bus around. It lumbers away with a puff of black smoke and a flash of taillight. And I'm on my own again. I walk past the parking lot and a gas station. There's a wooden barrier across the road, CONSTRUCTION ZONE. Traffic is turning aside, left and right. I keep going. The road keeps going too, but there's no one on it but me.

t's called the Queensway. A familiar name, like your best friend from the fourth grade, but it's been too long. I don't recognize anything about it. More of those yellow street-lights. Was a time when streetlights were white. I guess there's a reason why they changed. Under one of the lights is a bus stop and a bench. I sit down to rest but I don't feel comfortable. A big street with no traffic is an odd thing. Unnatural. I close my eyes. There's emptiness on one side of me, I can feel it. Cool, damp, earthy. A park. I rest awhile and think of emptiness.

Heavy footsteps come towards me. I get up right away. Heavy footsteps mean policemen with sticks saying, Get along. Like you were a dogie. Better to move without being told, it shows respect. Whatever a dogie is. Somehow I'm holding a handkerchief. I wipe my nose. The cloth is white, soft, faintly scented. I can't remember the last time I had a handkerchief like this. Actually, I can't remember this time. Where did I get it.

The footsteps get near enough for me to see who's making them. It's not a cop after all, but a big guy with crutches because his feet don't work. He stinks of glue. Not as bad as what was her name from St Pete's, but pretty bad. He passes by without saying anything. An angry guy, you can tell. Stomping with his crutches. Angry at everything. He won't get beat up much. Angry puts them off, Roscoe says. Be loud, he tells me, be something outside yourself, crazy or angry or happy or something. Whatever you are, don't be sad. Sad's a magnet, they'll kick a sniffle right down your throat. Roscoe's a bit of a poet.

I hear an unhappy sound from the litter basket at the side of the road. It's a cat, thin and raggedy, perched on top of the basket. It mews, reaching in and then pulling back. Hungry. I know how that feels. The cat reaches in again and I hear another sound. A baby crying. The cat draws back. The crying stops.

There's a baby in the litter basket.

I shout stop stop, at the cat, I guess. It darts away. I run to the basket. Green wire mesh, smelling of rot. I peer inside, paw through sticky cardboard and broken glass and I don't know what, and there she is, filthy and naked and so tiny I can put my hand around her waist. They threw her away because they thought she was dead, but she cries when I pick her up. A baby.

I examine her. No breath, no pulse. One arm comes off in my hand, and it takes me the longest time to fit it back on again. Her eyes open when she sits up and close when she lies down. She's cold. I wrap her in my handkerchief and button her into my jacket. She cries when I hug her. There there, I say.

I was tired. I'm not tired anymore. I start walking.

The moon sets, the streets close up, the trees whisper to each other about tomorrow, how windy it'll be, how bright, how much fun, and it's just a few hours away. I walk. The baby's been quiet for awhile now. I don't want to disturb her. I hope I'm walking in the right direction. The road squirrels around a bit. The construction zone ends, but there isn't a lot of traffic. I notice three reddish stars in a line. I try to keep them in front of me. Every now and then I trip or make a sudden movement and the baby cries quietly. I soothe her and tuck her back inside my jacket. She goes to sleep. Beautiful long eyelashes she has.

I'll take her to Sunnyside with me. They'll know what to do for her at the mission. Sally is a grandmother, and the other smiler, the dark one, Mary, keeps going on and on about her boy. I hope I'm walking the right way. The baby needs a bath and probably a change. So do I.

Daybreak comes from ahead of me. That's right, I think. I'm still on the Queensway. I don't know if that's right or not. My three stars turn out to be lights on a TV mast in the distance. They're the last ones to fade. Traffic picks up. Yawners, coffee drinkers on their way to work. Not local. This is a place to drive through, not a place to live. No signs telling you to walk, don't walk. No one walks here.

I can't decide what name to give the baby. They're going to ask when I get her to the mission and I'll have to know. I look around for inspiration, and I see a sign — BRIDGE UNDER REPAIR. I figure Martha would be better. SINGLE LANE TRAFFIC. Or maybe —

A car drives towards us very slowly. Lost, out of province. The license plate says, FRIENDLY MANITOBA. That does it, I tell her. Your name is Martha.

The sun's ahead of me, my shadow is behind. On my — left, had to work that out, is a grassy hill. The sounds of life are all around but softened by distance, squirrels and seagulls and cars going fast. I'm tired and starting to get thirsty. I don't walk as quickly now. Martha cries a bit. I wish I had something for her to eat.

The smell changes from dust and exhaust to water and exhaust. We're going downhill. Ahead of us is the Humber River. There's a bridge, but it's broken, and they're trying to fix it. The Humber is wide and dirty. Is it deep. I don't think so. I can see, what are they, bullrushes down by the edge of the water. We're nearly there, I tell Martha. Gulls are fighting by a chain-link fence. Why do they have a fence here, I wonder. KEEP OUT OF RIVER it says. But who would want to get in.

Wind blows downriver at me. Is that north. I think so. I walk on planks that shift under my feet. Through the slits in the wood I see the brown and busy water. It's moving fast, eager to get to Lake Ontario, sooner it than me. Big machines sit in the middle of the bridge. Yellow and fierce, giant animals with open mouths, ready to jump, but they don't. They're frozen in place, dinosaurs with an ice age coming down at the end of every shift. Traffic moves slowly, unhappily around them. The bridge is longer than I thought. When I look up I'm not even halfway across. And I'm not alone.

They slouch along, leather vests open, boots tied up tight. Music comes from somewhere near them. Their skulls are white all over except for bits of metal in their ears and noses and between their eyes. The metal glitters.

I keep walking. The music gets louder. I wonder about the music. Maybe they carry it on them somehow. Maybe it comes out of them like sweat.

They stop. There are four of them. They stand with their arms folded, blocking the makeshift sidewalk. They're smiling. Not infectiously. The leader speaks. You can tell who the leader is, the three guys give her a little space.

"And just where do you think you're going?"

Don't be scared, says Roscoe. But I am scared. I point across the river to the far side of the bridge.

She shakes her head. "That's Horsemen territory," she says. She points to a symbol that someone has spray-painted on the bridge. Maybe it's a horse. "We're Horsemen," she says and pulls up a sleeve to show me her bare arm. There's the symbol again, a black tattoo. The other skulls nod. They're Horsemen, too. They don't show me their arms.

"There's a toll," says the tall one in a loud voice. "In't that right, Beth. In't there a toll for passing through Horsemen territory?"

She nods. Hard to think of her as Beth. I don't ask how much the toll is — it'll be more than I can afford, whatever it is.

If I was alone I think I'd just go back, but I have to get Martha to a doctor. I take a step. Just one. The skinny Horseman with the knife moves fast. Before I can take another step he's beside me, his face inches from mine. He licks his lips like he's hungry. The tall Horseman is on the other side. His vest is covered with military medals and his jaw sticks out. The Horseman with the ugly skin rash and the yellow crusts around his eyes stays in front with Beth.

"Scary, huh?" she says. "Scared those fucking Sonix right out of High Park."

I'm scared too. I step back. The four Horsemen walk towards me. Famine, War, Pestilence and Beth. I'm tired. Martha lets out a cry. I don't blame her.

I don't see him reach out, but the tall one gets his hand on the front of my coat. "Look," he says, "a doll! He's carrying a doll around." I pull his hand off, turn to face him. Stay away from her, I say.

He blinks and takes a step back. Roscoe's right, anger puts them off. But not for long. They close in. I do what I can, spinning, kicking, spitting in someone's face and clambering over the barrier and into traffic. I forgot it was there. Couldn't hear it over the music. Help, I say, running alongside the cars, waving my arm. Help us, I say. The cars honk and squeal.

Horsemen are coming after me. I keep running until I reach the fence around the yellow monsters. Too high to climb, but there's a hole where the road sinks under the fence. I wriggle through. One of the Horsemen is right behind me. I kick, hear him grunt.

The yellow monster has places for hands and feet in the smooth sides. I climb. The music is louder. I reach the monster's brain, gears and levers and cracked dials, and suddenly I come face to face with Beth. She's already there, climbed over the fence, I guess. She grins and reaches out. I jerk back, almost fall, catch hold of something, and find myself on the shovel arm of the monster. There are holes in it, boot size. The big yellow beast has its shovel in the air. That's where I go.

You remember how the Ferris wheel used to stop to let other kids on. You'd work your way up the wheel, bit by bit, until your seat was the one at the top, and for a few seconds you were the tallest thing in the world, and you craned around trying to see everything, and your dad or your sister beside you kept saying, Be careful. Do you remember. That's what it feels like in the shovel. I peer over the edge. I don't know what I expect to see — crowds of people far below, balloons, mom waving. I see an orange pickup truck come to a halt inside the construction area. I see Beth. She's on the ground, not so far away after all. She's wearing her Beth's-head grin. And she's got Martha.

"Looky here!" she shouts, holding the baby up in the air.

Martha's crying. I know she is. Her blue eyes are wide open. I can't hear her over the music. Stop, I say. Oh God, make her stop.

Beth laughs, and twists the little arm around. Has she pulled it right off. Probably. I'm shaking, I'm so frightened. Stop, I shout over the noise. Leave her alone.

I don't care about the other three Horsemen. I don't care about the guys in hard hats getting out of the truck. They're looking this way. I don't care. Please don't hurt her, I say to Beth. Please. She smiles up at me.

"I had one of these dolls when I was a little girl. Cries when you squeeze it, right?" She squeezes. Martha cries. "That's right. Funny the things kids'll play with." Idly, without thinking, she tosses the baby into the river.

Out of the corner of my eye, in another life, I see the men in the hard hats. They aren't real. Beth is real. The river is real. I leap from the upraised shovel and land on top of her. Too surprised to move, probably. I knock her back against the what is its name. It's metal, about waist high, and stops you from falling into the river. The railing.

It doesn't stop us. I'm on fire, screaming, shouting, pushing. Beth doesn't move fast enough. Before I know what's happening we're both in the air, falling. Her skull face is pressed against mine. The music is all around us.

At six-thirty that morning I reached into a Caesarean incision and had my hand bitten. It was an emergency section, mom was under a general anaesthetic, and just as well because I jumped three feet in the air and shouted, "Holy Shit!" Not good for patient confidence. The child was born with all her teeth, a full head of hair, and no internal organs. And the morning continued as it started. Not a jewel day. An easy delivery — her fourth — hung fire so long we had to induce. What looked like a 5B cyst on the ultrasound turned out to be so big that we had to rethink the procedure, divert, graft, rebuild — and then, realizing we couldn't do it at the clinic, stitch her back up again and send her over to University Avenue. Everyone cut themselves. Needles and knives turned in our hands. People were late, equipment was unavailable and everything I did, every manipulation, every cut seemed fractionally wrong, as if I was working to a slightly different scale than my patients. Lunch, with an afternoon of looming paperwork, usually came too soon. Not today.

I didn't know it was my last clinic day. From my office I watched the sky filling with clouds, packing closer and closer, piling higher and higher, like teenagers in a phone booth. I had a sandwich I wasn't eating, coffee I wasn't drinking, and a journal I hadn't even opened. I felt as unsettled as the weather. I couldn't even enjoy the thought of the evening ahead.

I should have been looking forward to it. A young high-profile drug company with a reputation for aggressive research wanted me to chair a panel discussion on "The MD-Chemist." The proceedings were to be filmed for public television and written up in a California journal. It was a real boost for my reputation.

I sighed. Maybe I'd feel better in the limousine, or when the president of Pharm Trex introduced me as one of the nation's busiest and most respected obstetricians, but right now the whole evening seemed a little flat and out of focus. I couldn't get rid of the picture of the baby girl with the big smile and no insides. I pushed my sandwich away as the first bolt of lightning curved down, a giant fork to winkle the city out of its shell. Thunder followed close behind, and a torrent of rain. From my window I could just make out the lights of the bar across the street. I wanted a drink.

The downstairs was quiet and dark when I got home. Darling, I said, bounding up the stairs. No, that's not true. Bounding up the first two stairs, then trudging up the rest.

"We're in here," Lucy called from Cheryl Ann's room. I went in. Cheryl Ann was sitting up in bed. Lucy sat beside her with a thermometer in her hand. "Still pretty hot," she said.

"Time for more aspirin."

I took Lucy's place on the bed. So you have a temperature, I said. Good thing, honey, you'd be dead without one. She didn't laugh.

"Since this afternoon, daddy. They sent me home from school."

Let me get changed and I'll come right back and see you, I said. I shaved and put on my evening clothes, except for the jacket.

Cheryl Ann's face fell when she saw me. "You're going out," she said.

Lucy came in with the pills. "Remember? Daddy has an important dinner to go to tonight."

"But I'm sick."

"Don't be a baby," said Lucy. "I'll be staying with you."

I'm sorry, I said.

She smiled. "It's okay, dad. I remember about dinner now. You'll be on TV and everything. You should go.

I smiled back at her. God help me, I smiled and said, I'll look in on you when I get home.

"I'm hungry," she said. "Could I have scrambled eggs for dinner?"

"Sure." Lucy got up. "I'll make it for you right now. And some soup."

The phone rang. "That'll be him again," said Cheryl Ann, getting out of bed in a flash of pyjama and bare feet, and scampering into the hall.

Who's him, I asked Lucy.

"Leon — who else?" she said. "He generally picks her up after school but she wasn't there today. That's his third call since four o'clock."

We embraced then. "How was your day?"

Don't ask, I said. Her face tightened and she didn't ask. Doctors' wives tend not to. Honey, I made a mess of the Flinders' presentation doesn't sound as bad as, Honey, I made a mess of Mrs Flinders.

"Excited about tonight?"

Maybe a little, I said.

"I'm so sorry I won't be there."

And, I said, the ghouls and demons were about to fall on the Hero from a great height, with their skull faces and dreadful clutching fingers, when he heard a far-off sound, faint but welcome as a warm breeze in spring. It was the sound of a horse's hooves: clip clop, clip clop, and he looked up from his torment to see —

"Princess Cheryl Ann, coming on horseback." She smiled, her flushed cheeks dimpling. "And I was dressed in beautiful shiny pyjamas, glowing pink in colour, and over them a quilted bed gown with ruffled sleeves and a kleenex in the pocket. On my feet I wore magnificent slippers embroidered with the head of a famous talking mouse." We sat on the living-room couch. She squeezed my hand. My turn to smile. I could hear Lucy cooking, and the sound of CBC radio. Peaceful, timeless, domestic. I felt out of place in my cuff-links and dress shirt.

The demons were getting closer and closer, I went on, hurtling down from the sky at the speed of ultraviolet light. Would the Princess be in time, I said.

Cheryl Ann looked up. "But the Princess knew that time was an illusion," she said. "And that the Hero was not in worldly danger but in the thrall of enchantment. Wherefore she dismounted from her magnificent stallion and, bending low, kissed the Hero on the cheek. Like this."

And I — I mean the Hero awoke from his dream, I said, and beheld the Princess in her bed gown and mouse slippers, and his heart went out to her, for he could see that she had rescued him though she herself was sick of a mysterious fever. And he sought for and at last found the probing stick of mercury, and took the stick and inserted it under the Princess' tongue —

"Oh, daddy!"

The phone rang in the kitchen. We heard Lucy say, "I beg your pardon." Cheryl Ann relaxed. It wouldn't be Leon. "Do you want to speak to him yourself?" said Lucy. "Is there a problem?" I got up from the couch. "What — more important? Oh yes, I'll be sure to tell him." She hung up and laughed.

When she came into the living room a moment later, carrying a cup of soup carefully, her eyes were bright with amusement. "That was your ride on the phone." She put down the soup. "The car isn't coming. They asked if you could make your own way to the Inn on the Park, please. They did say please."

What's wrong, I said.

Lucy took the thermometer out of Cheryl Ann's mouth and looked at it. "Here, drink your consommé."

What happened, I said, to my ride.

"Someone more important needed it. I think that's what the man on the phone said. I had trouble understanding him. He sounded very worried. I suppose it's an organizer's nightmare: more VIPs than cars. I wonder who the someone is." She laughed again. "Kind of funny, don't you think, Mitch? You can ask around the dinner table to find out who they think is more important than you." Cheryl Ann spluttered into her soup.

I didn't think it was funny. I'd been looking forward to the ride as part of the evening's — I don't know — cachet. It was a symbol of how far I'd come. In taking the ride away they were spoiling the entire evening. It wasn't fair.

"I'm sorry, dear." Lucy was momentarily contrite. "I know it's inconvenient. Shall I call a taxi?" But she couldn't keep her face completely straight. "Or you could take the streetcar. Remember to get a transfer." Cheryl Ann spluttered again. I had a vivid picture of her telling this story to Leon.

Very amusing, I said.

"You're not really angry are you, darling?"

But I was. I'll be going, I said. I threw things into my pockets and left. I remember noticing Cheryl Ann's slippered feet on the coffee table. She wiggled them. It looked like Minnie Mouse was laughing at me too.

I wanted a cigarette but I'd forgotten my lighter. And I'd taken the keys to Lucy's BMW by mistake. I was too angry to go back in the house so I used the dashboard lighter and got out. No smoking in Lucy's car. I paced around the garage for a bit, kicking at the trash. Garbage bags, paint cans, strips of twisted metal left over from Lucy's Lady Macbeth. I'd have to remember to take it all out tomorrow. I climbed into the car, still angry, the cigarette clenched between my teeth. Halfway down the driveway I noticed that my window was open. I couldn't remember opening it. Driving one-handed, I took out another cigarette. To hell with Lucy's rule.

The guy from Pharm Trex was apologetic. He met me in the hotel lobby and led me to the Centennial Ballroom, exuding the wary *bonhomie* of a dog who's made a mess on the living-room carpet. He offered me drinks. He introduced me to people as "The man of the moment." He sweated and smiled and cringed and gradually I found myself in better spirits.

I knew some of the guests from similar functions and others by reputation. Doctors, lawyers, pharmacists, academics. I overheard somebody talking about parking problems and felt better — he hadn't been driven either.

"And now," said the Pharm Trex man, "you'll want to meet Ms Olsen." He led me to the centre of the room where Hanne Olsen, the blonde, striking, and famous head of Pharm Trex, was giving orders. I'd seen her smiling from glossy business magazine covers, read about her snarling in the boardroom. This evening was her idea.

"Camera one on the panel," she was saying to three or four scruffy note-takers, "camera two on the question microphone, camera three on the moderator. Who is he, anyway — some local scraper, isn't that right?"

My guide positively wriggled in embarrassment. "Ms Olsen, Ms Olsen," he cried. "Here he is. Please let me present our distinguished moderator." He introduced me in full, name, title, and all my academic qualifications. I felt silly. She turned, taller than I, superbly in command.

"Ah, doctor, we were just talking about you." A firm handshake. She stared over my shoulder and her face opened up.

"Poopsie!" Was she still talking to me. I turned and saw people scattering out of the way of a man in a chauffeur's uniform walking a leopard on a leash.

"Poopsie!" she called again. Not to me. She strode over to the nervous man and relieved him (literally — I'd never seen anyone look more relieved) of the animal. "Were they good to you?" she asked, stroking it. "Did they treat you nicely on the way over?"

Cameras rolled and clicked. I hung between anger and amusement for second, then the verdict came down. I burst out laughing. What a story for Lucy and Cheryl Ann: my ride had gone to someone's pet.

richard scrimger

My mouth is full of something strange. I can't breathe. I cough and cough. Water. I'm swallowing water. I'm lying in water. There's something holding me down, and water is rushing past me. I can't breathe, can't see, can't feel my legs. What I can do is choke and breathe in more water and choke some more. I haven't had so much fun in a long time.

I can hear. I hear something that sounds like gulls crying for help. I try to move. I can't, not even my head. I try again. I lift an arm out of the water, touch something metal. I pull myself up a bit. Not enough to matter. I try again, lifting my other arm and hanging onto the metal like a lifeline. It's slimy and cold but it's keeping me up. The gulls keep crying.

Can I pull myself higher. No. Again. No. I make one last try, and this time I pull myself up into a sitting position. Water runs against my chest.

I vomit, clearing my head and lungs at one throw. I'm weak as a kitten, can't move my legs, but I can see. What I am holding onto is an old shopping cart. Someone just tossed it into the river. Probably a kid. Kids have no respect for property. I'm sitting in water about a foot deep, me and this shopping cart and a lot of other garbage. The bridge is a long way upstream. I try to stand. Mistake. Pain goes right through me like green corn. I almost throw up again, it hurts so much. My legs are stuck.

I look over. One of the gulls is suspended in mid-air a few feet from me. His eye is alert, his mouth is open. He wheels away effortlessly and I notice the girl. She's turned against a big rock and her face is under the water. She's drowning. I reach out but I can't touch her. I let go of the shopping cart and push towards her. My legs don't work. I hold my breath and struggle with my arms.

How long does it take. Long enough to plant a seed, tend the plant, harvest it, dry it, send it to the factory to be cured and shredded and rolled into paper tubes, buy a pack, put one in your mouth, light and smoke it, and flick the burning stub out your car window like a miniature Catherine wheel. And drive away. About that long.

I reach the girl and turn her over. There's a bruise on her temple. She looks like she's sleeping. There are freckles on her broad nose. Beautiful eyelashes she has.

She's alive. She coughs up some water. I pull her towards me. Wires wrapped around her neck attach to a little radio. Horse tattoo on her bare arm. Only then do I realize it's Beth. I'm all set to drop her again, maybe push her out into the stream a bit, when she whispers something.

What, I say, pulling her closer, cradling her skull in my arms.

"Daddy," she says. Her eyes are closed. She isn't awake. Then she throws up on me. That's my girl. I don't let go of her, but I can't help throwing up too. The seagulls sound like they're laughing.

Voices in my ears. "Stay calm, fella." Hands under my shoulders, lifting me up. "We got you now. You're going to be all right."

Voices blending together. "Careful with her, can't tell what's broken. How do you feel now, can you hear us? What's your name? Where's the stretcher? What happened, anyway? They fell off the bridge. Oh, shit. See that, a rock must have done that. What's your name? Can you see my hand? It was just a few minutes ago, at the start of our shift, looked like they were climbing around on the back hoe. You're going to be just fine now. We're taking you to hospital."

I try to say thank you. Nothing comes out except water.

More voices. "There were a couple of others with the girl — looked like a gang. They ran off. The old guy's breathing okay. They both are. Let's get going. Good thing the hospital's so near. Okay, then."

Waking up is hard to do. I'm lying down with a drip in my arm and a light in my eyes. It's noisy all around me, groans and screams mostly. Every now and then someone says, "The doctor will see you in a minute." Sounds like a parrot.

The groans get louder. Whoever it is must hurt a lot. I'm so hot I'm burning up. My mouth is dry, and open. I close it, try to swallow. The groaning stops.

A girl beside me says, "I want drugs." She sounds tough and tired. "Goddammit," she says, "I'm lying here with my head strapped to a fucking board, staring at the ceiling, my arm's broken and my throat feels like a barbecue pit. Get me some drugs!"

Someone says, "The doctor will see you in a minute."

Is that you, Beth, I say.

"No, it's Mary Queen of fucking Scots. Who are you?"

I don't say anything.

"Are you the old guy who pushed me off the bridge?" she asks. "Are you the old guy with the doll? Are you?"

I don't say anything.

"Because if you are, I just want to tell you ..."

Yes, I say.

"I hope you're hurt real bad. I want you to hurt. You busted me up, you fucking gomer. Do you hurt? Do you?"

I swallow. Yes, I say. I hurt.

"Good."

Someone says, "The doctor will see you in a minute."

You know, Beth, you called me daddy. My eyes are closed. The light in the ceiling is too bright to stare at.

"What?"

In the water, I say. You were drowning, and I lifted you out and you called me daddy.

She snorts. "I haven't seen my daddy in years. I hate my daddy."

Someone says, "Are you awake now?" Are they talking to me. I open my eyes, but I can't see anyone. I groan.

Beth says, "He's awake."

Someone says, "We need to know your name, please. For our records. There wasn't any identification in your pockets." I tell someone my name. And of course that isn't enough. They want a whole bunch of other stuff I can't remember. I start shivering. They ask if I'd like something for pain. I say, Yes please. Like my mom told me.

They ask Beth too. She says "Yes, Goddammit."

Neither of us gets anything for the longest time.

was eating dessert, not paying attention to the chemist beside me, when I felt a sudden blast of intense heat. Bang. Right out of the air. The guy from Pharm Trex kept talking about his cure for stretch marks or whatever it was. My collar sagged with sweat. I blinked salt drops out of my eyes. My spoon slipped in my fingers. I felt as if I had just walked into a furnace. Furtively I looked around, but I seemed to be the only one affected. The ice cream in my bowl was still firm. I ate some. It didn't help.

I excused myself from the table. No one said anything. Nerves, I thought. I was worried about being on camera.

"Of course Poopsie eats ice cream," Hanne Olsen was saying a couple of tables away. "Vanilla is her favourite."

My face in the bathroom mirror looked sick and frightened. You're a doctor, I said to my reflection. What's wrong? I shook my head at myself. I didn't know either. Outside the bathroom was a pay phone, and on an impulse I dialled home. The line was busy. I dialled again. No answer this time. I let it ring and ring. No one picked it up. Had I mistaken the number, I wondered. I tried again. After ten rings I hung up.

"Doctor Mitchell?" It was my stretch marks friend from dinner. He was glad to have found me. "We were wondering where you were. The proceedings are about to begin. Ms Olsen is going to make her introductory speech."

I nodded. Coming, I said.

"Excuse me, but — are you feeling all right, doctor?" Of course, I said.

"That's good. Here, let me." He had a lighter out before I could stop him.

I pulled away from him. What are you doing, I cried.

"Lighting your cigarette." Christ, I didn't even know I had one in my mouth.

Thanks, I said weakly, I guess I'm a little nervous.

"That's natural." He clapped me on the back. "Don't worry, doctor. You'll do just fine."

Maybe I did fine. I don't remember much about it. Doctors and chemists gave arguments, asked and answered questions, appreciated each other's positions, nodded gravely. I took notes, kept order, summed up at the end. Mostly we talked in capital letters: about an Interdependent Relationship, about being Subordinate to the Patient, about Pure Research as the Hope for the Future. All very forgettable stuff. When it was over, Ms Olsen stood up and thanked everyone for coming. It's a wrap, she said. Have another drink. Poopsie yawned.

My tablemate congratulated me. "I told you," he said. "You looked totally relaxed up there. Almost like you were thinking about something else. Very impressive." I didn't reply. Premonitions are uncomfortable enough when you don't know what they're about. I knew. And that made it worse.

I stopped at the pay phone by the bathroom again. No answer at home. I tried another phone in the lobby. No answer. I called the operator.

"The line has been disconnected," she said.

But it can't be, I said. That's my home. I was just there, I said.

"I'm sorry, sir. Maybe you haven't been paying your bills."

The next half-hour was the most frustrating of my life. It was as if everything was conspiring against me, working to keep me from getting home. I know that Nature abhors a hurry; on the days you oversleep it will knot your shoelaces, spill your coffee, put your elevator out of service and make sure you hit every possible red light. Well, I was in a tearing hurry, so Nature made sure I couldn't even find my car. I waited on the front steps of The Inn on the Park, cursing the beautiful landscaping that surrounds the hotel while the parking attendant checked every car in the lot. We were about to phone the police when I remembered that I'd taken Lucy's car.

No, wait — a BMW, I said.

"What model?" I went blank.

White, I said. God, I couldn't remember what kind it was. Not too big, I said.

"License number?" I shook my head.

The parking attendant frowned. "First you tell me gray Cadillac. You tell me year, model, license, colour of upholstery.

You tell me everything about it except the engine number. When I finally prove to you it isn't here, you panic and shout out the first thing you can think of."

How many white BMWs are here right now, I asked.

He thought a minute. "Two," he said.

Let's check them out, I said.

The first one we came to was it. "You sure?" he said. I held out a twenty-dollar bill. He held out a familiar set of keys. I let out the clutch too fast and stalled the car, then practically ran the attendant down getting out of the lot.

The lights at Leslie and Eglinton were against me. I ran the intersection. The next one too, at Laird. All the way through Leaside and down the Bayview Extension I kept my hand on the horn, ignoring stop signs, driving faster than I should have, working the brakes and unfamiliar transmission very hard, shifting lanes constantly, overtaking on both sides, swearing at the other drivers, taking stupid risks that might gain me half a minute, as if the half-minutes would all somehow add up to a lifetime. Two lifetimes. And yet in the back of my mind, in a small dark place I was afraid to go, I knew. It was over and I was already too late. Driving like a maniac along the Gardiner Expressway was just something to do, something to occupy my reflexes, to keep myself from thinking before I had to. It was a way of not giving up, like pulling your goalie when you're seven goals down. I experienced flashes of hope, I saw myself walking up to them, embracing them; then fear returned, and the sense of loss, real and horrible, and as yet unacknowledged.

Sirens are a part of your life. You hear them every day. They are more real to us, more natural, than bees buzzing. But aren't they hard to ignore. Somewhere, someone is in trouble. Somebody's been hurt. Somebody's house is burning down. And it might be yours.

I was passing the empty public school when I heard it. The Sisters of St Joseph were thinking of turning the school into a mission house for derelicts, and the ratepayers were worried about property values. I swallowed, kept driving up Sunnyside, past the hospital with the new parking lot and the old statue, past streets named for girls long dead, Marion, Fern, Constance. The siren trailed away and I had a crazy moment of hope that the fire was someplace else.

I turned at Garden Avenue and drove slowly down the long curving boulevard towards the flashing lights and the noisy chaos of people and emergency vehicles. I felt sick. I stopped the car in front of the police barricade and got out. I could smell smoke and see the flames leaping. A policeman shouted something at me. I walked past him. He tried to grab my arm, but I shook him off and kept walking. The house was gone. I could see right through the front wall into the heart of the fire. Beams and supports stood out starkly, a charred skeleton of what had been a living home. Pumper trucks were busy hosing down the trees and the house next door. I didn't waste much time looking. I'd already seen Lucy and Cheryl Ann standing beside one of the trucks, wrapped in blankets.

I shouted and ran. They looked up. Were they as happy as

I was. Has anyone ever been as happy as I was. I couldn't laugh, couldn't cry, couldn't talk, I was so happy. All I could do was breathe and make odd squeaky noises. Leon stood behind Cheryl Ann. His face was blackened with soot. Lucy smiled and held out her arms to me. Her smile was a cup of sweet water and I was so thirsty.

"Welcome home," she said.

wake up and I'm sorry. I guess you're always sorry to wake up in a hospital bed. Unless you think about the alternative. I hurt all over, starting at my legs and going all the way up to my head. And I want a drink. Somebody groans.

"Is that you, doctor? Are you awake?" I turn my head. Somebody groans again. I guess it's me. It's dark. A senior nurse is standing there. Gray hair, sympathetic face. Her uniform is probably large size but it's still a little tight. She smiles.

"A pity you had to wake up. You looked so happy sleeping there." Oh, I say. I try to move, then wish I hadn't.

"Lie still, doctor," says the nurse. "Is there something you want?"

A drink, I say. She comes around the bed and offers me a sip out of a hospital glass with a flexible straw. I used to love those as a kid. Apple juice. I spill some. She wipes it up. Why do you keep calling me doctor, I say.

She smiles again. "I know who you are," she says. "You gave your name to emergency. And I saw you on the news yesterday. I wouldn't have recognized you, of course. Twelve years and a haircut will change anybody." She goes out. Who is she. She acts like she knows me.

It must be night. I can see three other lumps around me in the near dark. Two of them are snoring. I want a drink, and not apple juice. I try to remember how long it's been since I've had a drink. Never do this. It makes you sad.

I can move one of my hands. The other one is strapped down. I can turn my head. Freedom, except it hurts. Whatever I move, I feel pain. I wiggle my toes. It hurts. I blink. It hurts. Easier to keep my eyes closed.

"Shit," says the nurse. Not the one from last night. This one is young and disgusted. "What did you want to do that for!" She's holding a bedpan. She shakes it at me. "Couldn't you wait ten seconds," she says. Sorry, I tell her. The lumps around the room have stopped snoring. Two of them are arguing about whether it's cold in here or not.

"You've soaked past the pad and onto the sheet. Now I'll have to change your bed again," says the nurse. "And the doctor will be coming around any minute." I try to pull myself up a bit, make it easier for her. "Lie still, dammit," she says. "It's spreading all over the place." Incontinental drift. I lie still.

The doctor shows up for a moment, frowns down at me. "Oh, yes," she says. "You're the one." Am I. A cart with a squeaky wheel comes into the room. The lumps are eating breakfast. Another nurse does something to the tube going into my arm. "And this is your breakfast," she says, really cheerful. What does she want, a tip.

The doctor comes back, draws a curtain around my bed.

"How are you feeling this morning? I suppose your legs are still a bit sore." She pulls back the sheet. I nod my head. It hurts.

"Uh huh." The doctor frowns at my chart and mutters to herself. "Blood pressure, electrolyte imbalance, liver function impaired, A and B series positive. Oh dear."

What is it, I say.

"Just checking," she says. "You haven't been looking after yourself very well, Doctor Mitchell. Your legs should be fine in a few weeks, there's nothing broken. But I don't know about the rest of you." She looks inside my mouth, frowns and says, "Oh." Peels my eyelid up and says, "Oh." Listens to my chest and says, "Oh." Encouraging.

She frowns, thinking what to say to me. "Do you have any relatives," she asks after a moment. "Any close friends — someone we could notify?" If I didn't hurt so much I'd be worried. No, I say.

"Of course you could have picked up the hepatitis earlier," she's talking to herself again, "but you were in the Humber and the girl has it too. So it's probably a new load for the liver to carry. Damn. Tell me," she says in a louder voice, "do you want something for the pain? You shouldn't have to suffer." Sounds like she's going to have me put down.

How about a drink, I say, and not apple juice.

She opens her mouth to say no, then shuts it. "We'll see," she says. "It can't make much difference." She smiles but she's not happy.

The day passes like wind through a bulldog. I've had worse. I don't have to do anything except swallow and hold out my arm. I don't hurt too much anymore. I sleep long but not deep. Next thing I know it's evening and I have a visitor.

"Hello again." The big sympathetic nurse has a large paper bag under her arm. I say hello. The lumps in the other beds are arguing about macaroni and cheese. I didn't know you could. My arm is still full from dinner. The nurse closes the curtains around the bed, sits down and opens the bag. "Dr Fucik told me you wanted a drink," she says. "This is the best stuff I could find."

I can't sit up so I can't see what it is. She takes two tall glasses out of her bag, puts them on the table by the bed. There's a popping noise and then a fizzing noise, and the nurse says, "Here we are."

Outside the curtains I hear someone say, "And that's why they're called elbow noodles."

Someone else says, "They don't look like elbows."

"Do so."

My nurse friend cranks up my bed, grunting as she bends down. I stop hurting when I see the tall glasses filled with champagne. She gives me one, takes the other for herself. I thought this was for weddings and celebrations, I say. I hold on carefully. What are we celebrating, I say. Not that I mind.

The nurse blinks and looks sad. "Old times," she says. Sure, I say. I spill a bit, but get most of a mouthful. I start to choke.

"Are you okay?" She grabs my glass.

I swallow, choke a bit more, and nod. Yes, I say. Yes, I am.

"And the same guy invented the radio," says a voice from

outside.

"Did not."

"Did too."

"That was Marconi, you asshole. We're talking about macaroni."

"Who invented macaroni, then — Thomas Edison?"

Could I have some more, I say. The nurse smiles and pours. And suddenly I know who she is. You're Adele Creighton, aren't you, I say. She nods. Her eyes fill up. You were a nurse at the Civic Hospital, I say. You were with me that day.

"A lot of days."

Good heavens, how long has it been. When was the last time I saw you, I ask.

Her face tightens. "Just before your dismissal." Oh.

It's nice to see you again, I say. My glass is empty.

"You too." Adele refills our glasses.

You're all right, I kept saying to them. You're both all right. Are you both all right. The fire was nearly out. The garage was gone, and most of the roof, but the end of the house away from the garage was still intact. Looking up, I saw stars. The three of them took turns telling me about it.

"It was about nine o'clock and I was in the kitchen," Lucy said with a shiver. "Leon called to find out how Cheryl Ann was doing. I told him she was in bed and," she smiled at him, "to stop calling. Then I smelled smoke and heard these funny noises coming from the garage. I ran to the connecting door and — the whole place was on fire. In the middle of it I saw your car. I thought you were inside. I screamed. And then I heard a thud, and I turned around and — that's all I remember."

Cheryl Ann covered her face with her hand. "I was so scared," she said. "And so silly. Mom was down there in trouble, and all I thought about was myself."

"Nonsense, honey." Lucy was soothing.

"Some Princess," she said ruefully, looking at me.

I was so happy. The fire trucks blooped and gurgled behind us. The crowd milled around, chatting pleasantly, as if at a party. The smoke from the burning house gave a tangy barbecue odour to the night air. The hiss of the fire hoses and the crackle of static on the emergency radios, the shouts of the firefighters and the whine of the police sirens all faded into the background. I was even happy to see Leon.

"When I heard Mrs Mitchell's scream over the telephone, I got in my car and drove over as fast as I could," he said. "The garage was already going good when I got here. The front door was locked, and I had to bust a window to get in. It was real smoky. I found Mrs Mitchell on the kitchen floor. The line was dead — already burnt, I guess. I carried her out and went back for Cheryl Ann." He was matter of fact, the way teenagers are, but bursting with pride inside. And so he should be.

Go on, I said.

"I tied my sweater around my mouth, so I could breathe better," he said. "I knew I'd have to hurry. The hall was full of smoke, and I saw flames moving along the walls. I ran up the stairs to Cheryl Ann's room but I couldn't get in."

"I was so stupid."

"No you weren't," he told her, then to me, "she'd jammed blankets under the door, to keep the smoke out." I nodded.

"I guess I went a little crazy," he said. "I banged and hammered and finally broke down the door. The room was full of smoke — the blankets hadn't worked, the fire had come up through the floor, I could see flames along the baseboard, you know. I heard someone yelling for help. I didn't know where it was coming from at first. The window was open, and I thought she might be out on a ledge or something. We had a cat that used to do that, crawl out the window and then get stuck on a ledge."

Cheryl Ann smiled. "And you thought I was a cat?"

Leon shook his head. "I ran over to the window, and that's when I heard Cheryl Ann calling from inside the closet. I found her all curled up on the floor. I picked her up and carried her downstairs just before the staircase collapsed."

He stared at me, wanting my approval. I was too busy blinking back tears. When did the fire department get here, I asked.

He shrugged. "Ten, fifteen minutes later, maybe. I went across the street to telephone. The operator said someone had already called it in."

The noise ceased all at once — that awkward moment when everyone at a party decides to listen. Into the silence I said, Thank you, Leon.

"Forget it." He ducked his head and let me shake his hand.

Cheryl Ann started to shiver. Leon wrapped the blanket more tightly around her.

"Funny thing," she said. "I'm scared and shivery and I could sleep for a week, but I'm not sick anymore. I don't feel feverish and I don't have a headache. I feel better than this afternoon, really. Does that make sense, daddy?"

Fear, adrenaline, anoxia, relief — it's a potent combination, I said. But I don't think I can recommend conflagration therapy very highly. It may be effective, I said, but the side effects are pretty extreme.

Leon asked, "I wonder how the fire started?"

The fire department wondered too. Over the next few days they poked and prodded through the rubble of the house and our memories. I told the investigator the truth: I couldn't remember. I didn't have to tell him what I suspected. He already knew. He was a nice man with a notebook and he'd seen a lot of fires.

"I checked you out," he said. "You were at a big dinner uptown. Left in a hurry. Parking lot attendant said you were agitated. Having trouble finding your car. Your wife's car. That right?"

Yes, I said.

"You love your wife, doctor? And your daughter?"

Yes, I said. More than anything.

He took me over to what had been the garage. Now it was a wet, black hole in the ground. Still smelled smoky. "Nice big space," he said gently. "Not too many two-car garages in this neighbourhood. I understand from the blueprints that there was full electrical service here. It doubled as a workshop, your wife said. Paint cans, acetylene torch — she does some kind of sculpture, is that right? Did you get short-circuits, blown fuses, power outages of any kind?" I shook my head. He wrote it down.

"And what about you, doctor? Are you a handyman — rewire the bathroom, finish the basement, that kind of thing?" I shook my head. Mostly I went to the garage to be by myself, I said, and ...

"And what, doctor?"

And have a smoke, I said.

He closed the notebook.

We saw him off together, Cheryl Ann, Lucy and I, arms around each other, the burnt shell of the house behind us. The contractors were due tomorrow. He shook hands with us all.

"You know, doctor," he said, bending to climb into his car, "this may seem a stupid thing to say, but you are one lucky man."

I know, I said.

wake up clear and light, all my what do you call thems around me. Wits, I guess, but I'm thinking of another word. Whatever, I'm as sharp as I'm likely to get. I know where I am, and why. I can make out the clock on the wall and the headline in the newspaper someone left on my bed. CANADIAN TRAGEDY it says. Breakfast will be here soon. The lumps around the room are arguing about which is the best season of the year. They're having difficulty picking one. Winter's too cold, summer's too crowded, spring's wet and in the fall you end up with leaves in your pockets. And winter's coming.

"Good morning, doctor," says the nurse from yesterday. "Reading about yourself?"

Good morning, I say. She's smiling for once, maybe because I waited for the bedpan.

"Adele's been telling us all about you," she says. "How you used to be Head of Obstetrics at the Civic Hospital downtown, and about your tragedy."

One of the lumps brings up Christmas. "You mean winter," says one of the others."

"No, the Christmas Season," he says. "I look forward to it

every year. I think it's my favourite."

The nurse gives me a sponge bath, careful of the tube going into my arm. "That must have been horrible for you. Losing your family and then your job. And your own fault too."

"Christmas isn't a season. You might as well say baseball is your favourite season. Besides, what's so great about Christmas? It's cold and snowy."

I'm not really listening. I'm staring at the newspaper. Beside the headline is a familiar face, a woman with makeup and red hair and piercing eyes. Underneath is a picture of a ghoul behind a bunch of microphones. I know the woman. She's on the news. She has a hard handshake and a loud voice. I just don't know her name.

Is today Friday, I ask the nurse. It says Friday at the top of the newspaper.

"Sunday," she says. "Double time for overtime." Not today's paper.

"That article came out a couple of days ago. I read it. She's awfully good, don't you think? What's she like in person?"

Who, I ask.

"Christmas is when you feel good," says the lump who likes it. "Everyone feels good. And there's turkey for dinner. And presents. All the kids are so excited."

"But it's not a season," says the other one. "And when was the last time you got a present?"

The nurse plumps me down again, props the newspaper in front of my eyes. "Her, of course," she says. "Theresa Fusse. I read her column every week. She's on TV, too. Lots of people hate her, but I think she's great."

Theresa, I say. Yes, that was her name. But who's that, I say, pointing to the big picture of the ghoul. He's bald and bony, with dark eye sockets and a leer.

The nurse looks uncomfortable. "That's you."

She strides across the room, clean towels under her arm.

"I always get a present," says the Christmas lump. "Last year my Tina got me pants from where she works. And you know, I still remember my first hobbyhorse. I was so happy, I cried."

The other lumps laugh. The nurse tells them to be quiet. The cart with the squeaky wheel comes down the hall with breakfast for everyone but me.

I start to read about someone I don't know, an ambitious young doctor who attaches himself to one of the city's leading tycoon-philanthropists, plays all his cards right, and ends up with a fashionable practice and a seat on the Civic Hospital Board of Directors. Returning one night from a business dinner, he finds his luxurious West-End home in ashes and his wife and daughter burnt to death. Cause of fire: a lit cigarette carelessly discarded in the garage by the doctor. Six months later he is asked to leave the hospital. He never practices medicine again. His life in ruins, he sinks beneath the surface of the city, forgotten by all, to emerge twelve years later as the improbable hero in a fire rescue, "as if," writes Theresa, "with this one act of bravery he could redeem the past from the pawnshop of his memory, tear up the ticket with his guilt written all over it, and start afresh. What can we do for such a man except thank God that his lot is not ours, and buy him a drink. He's paid enough."

I don't know why the nurse likes Theresa so much. I don't like her at all. And I don't know what's going on. The guy I'm reading about, the stranger, has my name.

"Hello there," says my doctor. I look up from the newspaper. She's smiling. Does she get double-time too. "How do you feel today?" she asks.

Lousy, I say.

"You mean hung over? Adele said she'd bring you something. I'm glad you've got your spirits back. Nothing like a little complaining to show how you've ... improved." As she talks the doctor is drawing the curtain around my bed. She starts poking me, looking here and there. Have I improved, I ask, but she doesn't answer. I notice she's not smiling any more.

"There's nothing much wrong with your stomach," she says. "We can't take you off the IV because of the hepatitis, but you can try some real food. Does that sound good?" Ugh, I say.

"And I'm afraid we're going to have to move you. I've put in a request with the people at Our Lady of Mercy. It's a new wing of the hospital. One roommate, more light and a nice view of the grounds."

Am I all better, I ask.

"No," she says. "But we've done all we can for you here."

Lunch is meat, mashed potatoes, carrots, gravy. Gravy on everything, even the pudding. Unless that was the mashed potatoes. Adele comes by afterwards. She picks up the newspaper. "Did you read the article I left you?" I nod. I didn't eat much but I'm full. I could sleep.

Across the room they're asleep. Now that I'm sitting up they're not lumps anymore. I can see they're Blackbeard, Harelip and Tattoo.

"I brought the article because of what you were saying last night. About the fire. And your wife and little girl. You were drinking, not making much sense. I wondered if you remembered what really happened." I don't know what to say.

"I hope I did the right thing. I mean, if that's how you want to remember it, maybe you should. It's just that ... you were such a great doctor. I really liked working with you. And seeing you now ... I just thought you should know what really happened. I'm sorry."

Was I really a good doctor, I say.

Her face brightens. "The best I ever worked with. The best. You could do anything you liked in the OR. Like a magician. You used to say, 'It's another jewel day, Adele. We're going to save 'em all.' And mostly we did."

I smile. I can't remember it, but she can. That's nice. What happened to young Leon Opara, I say. The article doesn't mention him. You remember Magda's child, I say.

"No, I don't."

Come on, Adele, you were with me, I say. It was a long time ago, you were fresh out of school. It was pretty dramatic: a stillbirth who lived. Magda came in as a Jane Doe. Leon Opara himself adopted the boy, gave him his name. You were with me when he was born, I say.

She frowns. "You talked about a boy last night, how he saved your family in the fire. You called him Leon. Is that who you mean?" I nod.

"Do you want to know what happened to him? Really happened?" I nod again, but less eagerly. She sits down, takes my hand.

"Let me tell you, doctor, about a morning in the Civic Hospital OR a long time ago. A teenager named Magda was induced and gave birth. It was an easy delivery. You and I were the only ones in the room. She'd got her dates wrong, the fetus was twenty-six, twenty-seven weeks old. Should have been a stillbirth. But it was alive." I don't say anything. Adele wipes her eyes.

"I remember watching it breathe. I must have turned away a half-dozen times, thinking it was dead at last. But it wasn't. Somehow it kept breathing. We were both upset. Finally, you said you couldn't stand it any longer. You took a pillow and smothered it."

Light

"Are you all right, doctor? God, what did I do?"

Bright light and shadow. I'm choking. I see with two eyes, well I do, of course, but what I mean is, I see two worlds at once. One is shadowy, insubstantial, far away. In that world Adele is old and fat and very worried, checking my pulse and calling for help. And then, in a world of piercing clarity, I see another Adele, younger, holding a diploma in her hand and hugging her mom. Is that the real Adele. She's more real to me. I see my other nurse too, the young one, having a great time on the beach as the sun sets, her laugh louder than the surf. And I see her in the gray and distant world, a shade holding a needle. I feel her far-away hand on my neck, pinching. "Doctor Mitchell," calls Adele. "Come back, doctor, doctor. Doctor!" And the shadowy world returns big as before, big as life.

My neck hurts. My chest hurts. I have to pee. Oh boy. Good to be back.

Is he dead?" asks Blackbeard from across the room.

"You shut up," says Harelip.

"Both of you shut up," says my nurse. I have to smile. For a second there I saw Blackbeard in the light, the real Blackbeard, at his most alive, a ten-year-old discovering a corpse in the apartment next door. It's the best he can do. I'm kind of sorry for him.

Adele makes me drink something. She's sniffing and shaking her head, mad at herself. "I should never have said anything to shock you."

You're a good nurse, Adele, I say.

"Only thing I ever wanted to be."

Come and see me again, I say, and I lie back against the pillow, thinking of Harelip asleep in a tiny box-bed, smiling, secure as a four-year-old ought to be when tomorrow is Christmas and there's a hobbyhorse under the tree.

The doctor wakes me up. Of course. That's what doctors do. This one's a guy, haircut, shave, toothbrush, shoeshine, extra starch kind of guy. Hard to look at he's so clean. "Breathe," he says.

What, do I need a reminder. I breathe. "Again." He shines a light in my eyes, clicks his teeth a couple of times.

"I'm not comfortable," he says. I try to be sympathetic. Rough spot on a fingernail, doctor. New shirt catching you under the arms, maybe.

"Not comfortable about transferring you to the Mercy wing," he goes on. Oh.

"It's a long-term care facility," he says. "I just don't know how appropriate that is for you." What's he getting at. "I'd like to discuss your case with Dr Fucik, but she's off now and I won't be back at the hospital until Thursday and by then ..." his voice trails away.

By then what, I say, but he doesn't hear me. He shakes my hand.

"Well, nice to have met you, Mitchell," he says. A moment later the cart with the squeaky wheel comes with our dinner trays.

I don't touch mine. I don't feel like eating. And you know, I'm not thirsty. I lie back and close my eyes. Did you ever dream about someone else. It's an odd feeling.

The atmosphere in the hospital boardroom that spring morning was quiet and gray, like the suits on the three board members. They sat together on one side of the table. Mitchell sat across from them in a straight chair, as if he was applying for a job. He wasn't as nervous as an applicant, but then he didn't really want the job anymore.

The chairman put his glasses on the end of his nose and peered through them disdainfully. He'd never really liked Mitchell. A good enough doctor, but unable to take the larger view, somehow not board material — that's what he'd always thought. These days, of course, Mitchell wasn't even a good doctor. He was an embarrassment. He wouldn't be missed.

"Dr Mitchell's case reminds us of a painful truth," said the chairman. "I'm afraid that medicine is a highly stressful profession. The statistics are there for us to read. Doctors burn out."

Mitchell smiled grimly. A poor choice of words, Mr Chairman, he said. It was good to see the pompous old fart blush.

"I should have said —"

You'll be telling me I'm *fired* next, he continued. The new member, what was his name, lifted his pen from the sheet of foolscap and looked like a shocked schoolmarm. Opara was smiling.

"After a dozen informal cautions and two censures, one by the Medical Affairs Committee and one by the board," said the chairman, recovering himself, "the evidence is clear. Mitchell, your drinking has become chronic. You're a danger to your patients, to the profession and to yourself. You've resisted all our efforts to find help for you. You won't take a leave of absence. You have all our sympathy for your tragic personal loss, but we have to consider the hospital."

Mitchell said nothing. He'd had a drink to get up and another couple for breakfast, but his throat was starting to tickle. It was dry in here.

"A certain member of this board, to whom the hospital is already indebted for his selfless generosity," the chairman smirked obsequiously, "has persuaded the rest of us not to press for the revocation of your license. You should be grateful to him, Dr Mitchell."

Leon Opara considered the bleary, tousled figure. Poor Mitchell. He didn't look grateful. He looked like he'd already resigned. The old man remembered their last lunch together. They'd had a lot to drink and Opara had tried to talk some sense into him. "Put grief behind you and get on with the job, man. You used to be a fine surgeon. The kind other surgeons talk about. Doesn't that mean anything to you?" Mitchell had shaken his head and reached for his wine glass.

The chairman, bloody man, hadn't finished yet. Opara sighed, regretting the impulse that had brought him here today. At this rate he'd never get to the Municipal Board meeting before lunch.

"It is my painful duty to inform you, Dr Mitchell, that as of this moment your hospital privileges are revoked. You may not enter any of our facilities in a professional capacity. A notice to this effect will be circulated from the office of the President. Do you have anything to say?" Mitchell shook his head.

"Very well. That will be all, doctor."

The boardroom doors needed oil. They creaked as they shut behind him for the last time. Mitchell walked down the familiar corridor to his office, got his coat and went to the parking lot as if it had been any other weekday these past ten years. He stopped when he saw Lucy's car in his parking spot.

He still thought of it as the wrong car. The Cadillac was fire-blackened scrap metal. Probably already been melted down in one of those giant cauldrons, sold to Westinghouse and turned into dishwashers or something. He got in the small white car, stalled the engine, restarted and stalled again. He hated the car going dead under his fingers like that. He gunned the motor before sliding it into gear and kept his foot on the gas so the car wouldn't stall again. Someone in his way, he threw the wheel over and kept going. Instinct, it was all instinct. Things happened and you did what you had to do. Traffic led him south, then east. There was a mickey of vodka in the glove compartment.

He kept driving. The alcohol spread throughout his body, warming the cold places, clearing the foggy places. He knew where he was now, and what he had to do. Roaring down

University Avenue in the glow of the yellow street lamps, where had the day gone, where had all the days gone, hand on the horn, passing by late-night traffic as if it was standing still. Faster, faster, he had to get back. Even though it was too late, he had to get back.

Mitchell got off the expressway at Jameson and drove carefully along King Street, slowing to a stop for the red light at the Queensway. He yawned and wriggled his toes inside his dress shoes. He was looking forward to telling Lucy all about the evening. She'd get a kick out of the Poopsie episode, and the memento from Pharm Trex — a bronze prescription pad with his name and the date on it — which sat in its presentation box on the passenger seat. Really, who thought of these things. The dashboard clock blinked 10:30, five minutes fast. Lucy liked it that way; said it kept her from being late.

He'd always been fond of the ride up Sunnyside Avenue, with the lake behind him, past St Joseph's, which presided over the neighbourhood with prim old-world dignity, rather like the Sisters who still ran it, past the tall narrow houses with their small swept front lawns and well-tended gardens, past the shade trees and quiet cross-streets leading over to High Park, past the school and the United Church, past all the people with their dogs and groceries and cigarettes and bicycles. Sunnyside was a street of re-entry for him. It was the way home.

Not tonight. His sleepy side-street was blocked by fire trucks and crowds of people. He got out of the car and ran.

Neighbours saw him, pointed, turned away. He splashed through puddles, dodged uniforms and equipment, got near enough to see nothing, no one, cried out, grabbed the nearest arm. The noise was incredible.

"Get away!" shouted a busy firefighter.

Where are they, where are they, he screamed.

"Stand back!"

The ambulance was parked by the side of the road with its red roof light circling and the rear doors open. Mitchell dropped the firefighter's arm and ran over. Two black bags with zippers running down their length lay on the grass like the trash for tomorrow's collection. Standing beside them was a stranger with a white coat and a clipboard. Bile rose at the back of Mitchell's throat. The bags weren't secured. He knelt, fumbled with the zippers. The white-coated stranger made no move to stop him.

Who are you, Mitchell asked.

"I'm the Examiner."

The Medical Examiner. Oh God, he said, then they really are dead. They're both dead.

"I'm sorry, doctor," said the Examiner.

And our home is burnt down, said Mitchell. He was still on his knees. We came here when we got married. Never wanted to move, he said.

The Examiner nodded.

How did it happen, Mitchell asked suddenly. What went

richard scrimger

wrong. Where did it start, he said.

"The fire?" asked the Examiner. As if there was something else.

Why couldn't they — gesturing to the fire trucks — have got here in time. Mitchell was shouting. Or me. Or someone. Why couldn't someone have got here in time.

"Someone might have," said the Examiner, "only —"

Only what, he said.

"Only he's dead. Do you remember?"

wake up and it's time. I know. The clock on the wall says something, so does the watch Adele wears on her chest. They probably say the same thing. I don't mean that time. Adele says hello.

I need a wheelchair, I say.

"What's going on?" she says calmly. "Where are you going, doctor?" Where does she think, Bangkok. "There's no rush to get out of here. You may not get to the Mercy wing, but no one wants to put you out on the street yet."

I'd like a wheelchair, I say. I won't be able to walk. Could you get me a wheelchair right now, please. And some blankets, I say. My voice is urgent. Somehow I make it an order, doctor to nurse.

"I remember seeing a spare one down the hall in 4D," she says.

Get it, I say.

The chair is broken-backed and one of the front wheels won't turn properly. I settle myself in the blankets. Let's go, I say.

"I don't think you're fit to go anywhere," says Adele quietly.

Yes I am, I say. I push as hard as I can. The chair makes a slow quarter-turn. I look up. She's smiling. So are the guys in the other beds. Very funny. I push again. The chair moves ahead maybe six inches. Please, Adele, I say.

"Oh, all right." She takes hold of the chair. Thanks, I say. I'm tired.

"See you around, doc," says Harelip. He waves, a friendly gesture.

Goodbye, I say. Have a merry Christmas. It's too early for Christmas but he knows what I mean. He smiles his twisted smile. Adele gives the chair a push. It takes us two tries to get through the doorway.

We move two squares forward and one to the left, like a what is it on a chessboard. Good thing the hall is empty. A bell rings and a voice tells us that visiting hours are over for today. Thank you for coming, says the voice. Travel safely. You'd think it was a cocktail party.

Adele wrestles the chair around a corner. The elevator door is closing. Wait, I call, and someone holds it open for us. Ground floor, I say. And thank you.

In the elevator another nurse notices Adele. "I thought you were on days now," she says.

We stop at the third floor on our way down. Maternity. Lots of visitors in maternity. There always used to be, I remember. Same smells too, shit and milk and sweat.

"Doctor? Doctor?" Adele is kneeling beside me. "Are you all right, doctor?"

What, I say, yes, I'm fine. I take a deep breath.

The night air is cool and fresh. Feels like it just stopped

raining. The sidewalk ahead of me is practically empty. Just as well. The wheelchair moves like a dodge 'em car.

Adele shivers. "Let's get you back to the ward," she says.

I shake my head. I can't stay. Headlights flash across the sign behind me. ST JOSEPH'S HOSPITAL. SUNNYSIDE ENTRANCE.

"Dr Fucik will be upset."

No she won't, I say. Neither will anyone else. I'm a problem that solved itself — a short-term problem at that.

"I'll be upset."

Don't be, I say. And anyway, I have to go. It's time.

Maybe she understands. She doesn't stop me. "Where are you heading?" she asks.

I point down Sunnyside. Home, I say.

"You're not going to get very far."

How do you know, I say, how far I'll get. She nods, blinks, sketches a tentative wave. She understands.

I look back. She already seems a long way away. "Goodbye," she says, her words floating in the air like winter breath. I see them before I hear them. Speed of sound. Goodbye. Goodbye. I push on the wheels of my stupid chair. Good thing I'm heading downhill. I wonder, will they be glad to see me at the mission, what is his name and what is his name and Roscoe. And the smilers, the kindly ones, Sally and Mary and the others. I've missed dinner. Probably get there for lights out. Tomorrow I'll scrounge a cup and set up on a nearby corner. Show off the bandages on my legs. Nothing like a bandage for sympathy.

Help me back on my feet, mister, I'll say. Thanks. Have a good day, mister.

The sidewalk stretches out ahead of me like a ribbon of dirty gray silk. In the distance I can see inky water and moonlight shimmering. That's the lake at night, days it's as gray and dirty as the sidewalk. Time and traffic rush past me, full of their own concerns.

Disaster strikes with its usual banality when the chair rolls off the sidewalk and a wheel gets stuck in somebody's front garden. Neat little house with a railed porch and dark-coloured front door. I can't move. I sit there like a stranded sea creature, waiting for someone from *National Geographic* to rescue me. I hear a big engine behind me and turn around in time to see a bus. Its destination flashes like a beacon — OUT OF SERVICE. That's right, I remember. There are no buses on Sunnyside.

The front door of the house opens and light spills out like crude oil from a ruptured tanker. A man steps towards me. There's light all around him and I can't see him. "You look like you need some help," he says. "Can I give you a push?"

Thanks, I tell him. And sorry about your flowers.

He's a sturdy older man with a beard. Something familiar about him. He's smiling at me. "Hello, Mitch," he says.

I open my mouth to ask who he is, and then he puts on the fur cap he's got in his hands. The light around his head dims and it's my friend Joe. I never saw him without the cap before.

"I told you I'd see you again." He takes hold of the wheel-chair and eases it back onto the sidewalk. "Remember?"

You're looking great, Joe, I say. I don't tell him I thought he was dead. Do you live at that house, I say.

"No no. I was just waiting there." He pushes me on a bit. "Is this the way you're going?" he asks.

Sure, I say. Thanks, Joe.

We make pretty good time. Before I know it we're at the foot of Sunnyside Avenue, beside the what do you call it, the little roundabout for the Queen streetcars. There's one there now, empty except for the driver. She's changing the sign at the front. CROSSTOWN SUNNYSIDE becomes CROSSTOWN NEVILLE PARK. The driver settles into her swivel chair with a newspaper and a cup of coffee.

The far side of the Queensway is a bluff overlooking the CNR tracks, the Gardiner Expressway and the Lakeshore Boulevard. Before they built the expressway you could take Sunnyside Avenue or Indian Road right down to the lake. Nowadays the only way is a spiderweb-thin pedestrian bridge with rickety green railings. That's where Joe pushes me. It's very windy. Joe stops to tie the fur cap under his chin. We keep going while trains and cars roar beneath us like a river of light and smoke. The bridge is swaying. Where are you taking me, I shout. Is this the way. Joe nods calmly, keeps pushing.

On the far side of the bridge a switchback ramps leads down to the ground. Joe takes it slow. The air starts to get brighter and hazier at the same time, as if we're driving into fog with our high beams on. It always is a bit misty right down by the lake. I can't move. I can hardly breathe. The ramps are steep. I'm practically falling out of my chair. Joe has to hold me in. I want — it's the strangest thing — to *push*. How often have I heard women say that. Joe says we're nearly there. The blur of light is pressing all around me. It isn't fun exactly, it's too exciting and scary, but I don't want to turn around, and anyway, you can't climb back onto the diving board after you've jumped.

We get off the ramp, but I still have the urge to fall forward out of the chair. The fog hangs close and damp and still, and when it blows away all I see is more fog. Joe takes me a little way and then stops. A building looms out of the murk. Plain white clapboard with green trim. The Palais Royale.

Joe offers me a hand. Without thinking, I take it and find I can stand up. My legs are still bandaged but I can walk up the steps. Thanks, Joe, I say, turning around, but he's gone.

There's a bouncer on the doorstep, got a set of keys in his big stone fist. I can't believe it, it's my friend Pete. Hey Pete, I say, nice to see you back together again. Still got that birdshit problem, eh, Pete. He doesn't say anything.

All kinds of stuff going on inside the Palais Royale. The place is shaking.

Can I go in now, Pete, I say. He doesn't open the door. I wonder if maybe he hasn't heard me. I point at the door. Can I go in, I say. He just looks at me. Not a great talker, Pete, he never was.

The door opens. A great white light shoots out, and a noise like a hurricane. I have to close my eyes. When I open them the door is shut. Pete's still there. He stares at me and I begin to understand. It's not a question of seeing clearly, seeing isn't as important as it used to be. More like a memory, but not quite my own memory, if you know what I mean. No, of course you don't. Pete's beard moves. Maybe he's smiling.

And then I see them. I run towards them, waving like a madman and crying. They're crying too. They're smoke-grimed and dirty, their clothes are scorched. They look great. Lucy's wearing her yellow housecoat. The hair's been burnt away from one side of her face. Hi there, I say. She smiles and sniffs. One of Cheryl's Minnie Mouse slippers is missing. She holds the baby, little Leon, who didn't save her after all. He's small enough to fit in the crook of her arm. Oh, Cheryl Ann, I say, I'm so glad. I can't say any more.

Lucy and Cheryl Ann have tickets in their hands. I don't. My hands are empty. Cheryl Ann holds the baby out to me. "He's got your ticket, daddy," she says. I'm trembling as I take him. He's waving with one hand. The other is in his mouth. Sure enough, he's chewing on the ticket. I take it away gently. Thanks, Leon, I say. I guess he doesn't need a ticket. He clutches my finger for a moment and gives one of those baby smiles. Gas, probably.

The big door opens again. I'm scared and excited. Leon doesn't care. He's blowing bubbles. The door closes and it's misty dark again. Cheryl Ann is holding hands with a frail old woman. I didn't see her before. Hi there, I say. Her fine wrinkled face is lit up like Saturday night. "And what happens now?" she says. Good question.